SUMMER CAMP FOR WEREWOLVES

DAMIEN CASEY

ISBN-13: 979-8-9933182-2-6

To Dee Wallace - Thank you for going to the original summer camp for werewolves.

Chapter 1

The 5 O'Clock Report Has Got Nothing On Me

ANY REPORTER WORTH THEIR weight in salt will tell you it's super important to get out of your comfort zone. Do you think Connie Chung became a household name by playing it safe? Did she only write stories about cats in trees? Did she never leave her hometown?

I'll be honest with you.

I don't know.

I did a report about her in the fifth grade, and I've forgotten most of it. I'm a freshman... well, I guess a sophomore now... at Colony High School, and I'm usually too busy with the mountains of homework the teachers give us to have any time to sit around and pleasantly reminisce about how nice things were in elementary school.

Oh, to have recess again.

Thanks to my new problem, I really could use recess.

More on that later.

That's another thing about a good reporter. They never give away the best bit. If a reporter is bad, they will give you the whole story in the first column. I want you to see "turn to page A7 for the rest of the article." I want to leave you with something so interesting you turn to page A7 and physically cannot stop for the comics page. If this were the nightly news, you wouldn't channel surf during the commercial break; too much risk of missing every word of the story.

I was eight when I realized this was my life's dream. She had a black blazer, curly red hair that was so big you could sneak a buffet into a movie theater inside of it, black pants, and pink cowboy boots. There was something about those boots that fascinated me. She was so put together and professional that I would have believed she owned a bank; but those boots told me that maybe she owned it because she robbed it. We were on our fifth-grade field trip to Columbus, Ohio. We were visiting this museum where you could ride a bicycle across a high wire in the middle of the building. The death-defying bicycle held up by physics seemed boring in comparison to this woman talking to everyone she could. She never stopped; she was a social butterfly covered in smiles. She was like a conversational lamp bringing in all of the shy moths.

You get it.

Sorry, I get a little flighty when I write.

I have always been shy. My mom has accused me of being so shy that I would make a really good cryptid. I didn't know what she meant, so I looked it up one day. Very funny, Mom.

This woman wasn't like that. She was sad when she wasn't talking to someone. You could literally see the energy drain from her body when she wasn't yapping. I wanted to be like that. If I could have one superpower, it would be to make everyone feel talkative. Super-friend-girl or something. Really, I love people, and I wish I could talk to them more. It turns out that talking to people is a super crucial part of being a reporter and making friends.

I followed her around all day; she started to call me her little assistant. I didn't talk to her still. No way. The cameraman even let me hold the camera for a little while; I couldn't even say thanks. I just followed her and listened to her talk to kids about how fun this place was. She even did an interview on this piano that you had to walk on to play! It was amazing!

"Hey," she said to me after I followed them to the exit of the museum. "You probably shouldn't go with us. Your parents and teachers would freak!" Her voice was southern. When I say southern, I mean the kind that you would see in a movie where everyone wears a button-up shirt. The movies with a lot of denim, fishing, and people with two names like Bobby-Sue. She walked me back, patted me on the head, and turned to her cameraman.

"Hey," she said, fixing her blazer. "Want me to interview you?"

I nodded my head.

Of course I did!

"When we start recording, I'll just ask you what your name is, and what you want to be when you grow up. Is that okay?"

I nodded again, trying to find the courage to talk. In my head it was as if words were currency, and I didn't want to waste all of my money on chocolate before I could get a new comic.

"Hello, Columbus!" As soon as she started talking, the world lit up. I was fine, I wasn't afraid to talk anymore. Being in close proximity to those cowboy boots really helped me. That must be how she had her power and just being near them was affecting me in a small way!

"I'm here with another student traveling to COSI. She's a cute little thing too! Why don't you tell me and the people your name, and what you want to be when you grow up?"

I froze because of course I did.

I sighed, knowing I had ruined my whole entire life right there on TV. People in Alaska would see this; I wouldn't even be able to go live a life of solitude in the frozen tundra. I would be out fishing when all of a sudden, a polar bear would say, "hey, there's that girl that totally blew it on live TV!" The bear would probably take pictures then. Polar bears do carry around cameras; it's a super rare trivia fact.

Tangent about bears with cameras aside.

I looked at her boots and felt the power. I could do this.

"My name is Marsha White," I said. "And I want to be a reporter!"

"Wow! A girl after my own heart. You'll be stealing my job one day kid!"

I don't know why she did it, but she picked me up and sat me on her shoulder. I don't know how she did it with one arm, but I knew she had to be able to. She was a superhero after all so why couldn't she pick up a little kid?

"And with that," she said. "Thank you for tuning in, Columbus. Anne Ambrose hoping you've had a good dinner and aren't missing bedtime!"

She sat me down, hugged me, and gave me a pin the size of a quarter from her jacket pocket. It had her face, her name, and her TV station in pink with a white background.

"I don't give these out much," she said. "But you deserve it."

I wear that pin on my denim jacket still to this day.

She gave me a hug, waved goodbye, and left me with the class I came with. I don't know how she knew that was my class either. I chalk it up to assuming a misplaced little kid will make her way back to the kids she's supposed to be with… but honestly, I know it's because she's some all-knowing entity that was sent to save me from the boredom of watching kids ride that dumb bicycle. I know, I know, but really, see it one time and you're good!

I didn't want to go hang out with my class. I had watched the class clown, Jack Kessler, pretending to eat his boogers for ten minutes on the bus ride here. Jack is still annoying, unfortunately Jack is the only person who wants to talk to a girl who barely talks back. He's sort of my default best friend… I guess.

He doesn't do the booger eating thing anymore because he's more interested in the new girl, Jennifer Stirba.

Let me clear that up, she was the new girl, that was the middle of last year. She's the source of all my new problems.

I'll get to that, I promise.

Jennifer, or Jenny, or Jen, or "whoa..." depending on who is talking, is tall and blonde. She looks exactly like every girl that every annoying high school boy that used to pretend to eat boogers would be totally in love with. When she first moved to our hometown, Cohen, Ohio, I made faces at her behind her back all day. She was the kind of person Anne was, and it bothered me. People gravitated to her; she was the sun and everyone else was waiting for her to decide if they would be a planet or moon in her galaxy. That was supposed to be my role in the public school ecosystem.

At the end of the year, I had my fill. Jack and I had waited all year to go see the new Godzilla movie after the last day of school ended. We would walk home, Mom would make us one of her famous Hawaiian pizzas, and then we would go to the theater. I'm lucky, I live just two blocks from the movie theater. If I get bored, I can gather together enough change and go see something. My dad is a bit of a space movie nerd; I don't mean good ones either like *Star Wars*. He likes these really dumb ones where the spaceship is basically a painted cardboard box and there's always some woman wearing silver shooting lasers at monsters made of clay.

It's not a very college science professor of him thing to like, is it? But I guess maybe those movies are his Anne Ambrose in a way, so I let it slide.

Jack asked if it would be okay if Jenny came to the movies with us. Apparently, she loved giant monster movies and had a complete VHS collection of Gamera. Okay, I can admit it, that's really cool... but not cool enough to steal the only friend I have!

I said "no."

Only I didn't just say "no."

I took a signed picture my dad has from some actress from a movie called *Battle Beyond the Stars* and put it in front of my face like a mask. I then walked around in front of Jack talking about how sweet, cool, and pretty I was.

I wasn't really proving a point other than why Jack would want her to go with us.

Jack decided two could play at that game and picked up another one of my dad's signed pictures. This one was for that dumb Jane Fonda movie I refuse to watch. He started making fun of me by just not saying anything and walking around with the face as a mask.

It was pretty funny, and I was happy he chose that picture. My mom always said I looked like her. I liked that compliment so much that I started styling my hair the way she did in *Klute* when I was in seventh grade.

My mom thought that was cool.

My dad said it was very progressive of me.

I just think it's a good haircut.

We laughed off the insults and went to the movie.

Yes, Jenny was there.

No, she wasn't as terrible as I remember.

Actually, she was pretty cool.

The movie, I don't know, maybe people will like it in thirty years.

It was dark when we left the theater. It was muggy and warm, just a typical Ohio evening in a river town. You could feel the moisture in the air, and it made everything feel like a warm bath. Old people always say, "It's not the heat that'll geetcha, it's the humidity."

Jenny said her parents were at a friend's house down the street and left in the opposite direction.

Jack was ranting about how Godzilla didn't even look like Godzilla. How his roar didn't even sound like Godzilla's roar. I wasn't too worried about that; sometimes Superman looks different too and people don't complain.

"SKKRREEEEOOOOONNNKKKKKK," he yelled at the top of his lungs to make sure I remembered what Godzilla sounded like. Boys are always explaining things to girls that girls already know. I think they enjoy the sound of their own voices. I don't think Jack needs to tell me that the singer of Oingo Boingo is Danny Elfman's brother every time I wear the shirt, but he does.

"SKRREEEEOOOOONNNKKKKKK!" He yelled again.

"HARRROOOOOOOOOOOOOOOOOO!" something responded.

"No," Jack said. "Good try, Marsha. But Godzilla does not sound like a werewolf."

"ARRROOOOOOOOOOOOOOOOO!" The voice yelled again.

"I'm telling you," Jack said. "I like that you're talking more... but that's just not right at all."

"Jack," I said. "It wasn't me."

As soon as I said it, a figure appeared before us on the sidewalk. It stepped out of the tall bushes between the two houses and stared at us. The streetlight was behind it so we couldn't make out who or what it was. All I could see was the silhouette. It was seven feet tall, it had long spindly limbs, its arms and legs were faintly muscular, there were two pointy ears on top of its head. It smelled so bad; I'll never forget it. It was a mix of wet dog and burnt wood.

It fell forward on all four limbs and ran toward us. We turned and ran as fast as we could, screaming all the way. The thing nipped at my foot and bit into my heel a little bit which sent me flying face first like Superman learning to fly (in his normal outfit so not to make anyone get picky). I landed stomach first on the ground. The only thing that stopped me from smashing my face into the concrete was Jenny's pink Fila shoes.

"Get out of here!" she screamed at the beast. "Go home, Marty!"

I closed my eyes because I didn't want the last thing I saw before I died to be faded pink Fila's. I could hear whatever it was behind me breathing. It was growling low and slowly approaching us.

"Marty, I'm not joking," Jenny said as calm as a math teacher handing out a pop quiz. "If you don't go home right this very instant... I'll tell mom you got loose. You know how mad she'll be. Downright pissed."

I could hear the embodiment of death taking a few steps backward. Its breath slowed down, and it stopped growling.

"Marty, I am not kidding around here," Jenny said as she took a step forward. "GO HOME!"

When she yelled that time, she lifted her hand like she was going to strike. I don't know what kind of witchcraft Jenny is working with, but I need an ounce of it because that... thing... ran away whimpering in fear.

"Sorry about Marty," she said as she helped me up. "He's not a good dog. He was until the vet gave him the wrong medicine. Now he's really temperamental all of the time. Can't even give him a treat without him being mildly annoyed."

"*That* was a dog?" I asked, the fear forcing the words from my mouth.

"Yeah. A German Shepard actually. My dad used to be a police officer before we moved here. Marty was his K-9. He got injured when a burglar broke into our house. That's how dad got hurt too. He had to retire."

"I'm sorry. That has to suck."

"Living with Marty? No, it's okay! He's really sweet with me. That's why he's afraid of me hitting him. He's righteously afraid of mom though. I mean, who isn't?"

"Yeah... ha."

If Marty was afraid of Jenny, and Jenny was afraid of her mom... I didn't want to meet her mom anytime soon. I don't think anyone would try to tell her what Godzilla sounded like.

"What was that?" Jack said. He stepped out from around the corner he ran around. Some bravery, Jack.

"Oh, no," Jenny said. "You're bleeding a little. He doesn't have rabies or anything like that, so let's go to my house and my mom will clean it up. She's a nurse!"

Oh, cool, I thought, *I'm going to meet the scariest thing alive.*

"What's your mom like?" Jack asked. He must have over-heard the conversation and wanted reassured that maybe she wasn't as scary as Jenny said she was.

"She's totally cool!" Jenny said. Her smile grew, and that was enough reassurance for me. She was happy to take us; that's not what people who live with Jason Voorhees do.

We walked down the street with the promise of a phone to call home from and threats of Ale8 brought from Kentucky last weekend.

That was the first time I saw a werewolf.

Turn to page A7 to read more.

Chapter 2

A7

"YOU MUST NOT LIKE my daughter very much, do you?"

Okay. So not only was Leslie Stirba the scariest person walking on planet Earth; but apparently, she was also an IP - Intuitive Person. What was I supposed to say here? I felt like honesty was not the best policy, and she was bound to destroy me physically and emotionally if I said what I thought of Jenny. So, I stuttered, looked around, picked at my fingers, and shrugged.

What a chicken.

We didn't even have time to really get the vibe of what was going on in that house. It was a two-floor house, the kind of place that kids sneak out of the second floor from using a vine covered tresses... I'm not one hundred percent sure that's what they're called, but I'll roll with it.

Just your basic white picket fence American home.

We walked up a small set of stairs and into the living room. I'm always fascinated by which door people use to enter their homes. It says a lot about what that person values the most. For example: my dad enters our house through the door in our living room; all of his movies and posters and other junk are there to greet him. My mom enters in the kitchen; she went to culinary school and now runs a kitchen in this upscale spinning roof restaurant; food is her passion.

If I could enter my house in any door, I would have a doorway into my closet because that's where I keep all of my favorite newspapers, magazines, and VHS tapes of news segments I wanted to remember. Yeah, I'm a nerd about it. How am I going to get good at something if I don't consume excessive amounts of it? At least that's what my mom says about all of the cheese she eats.

Inside the Stirba home, Jenny's dad was placed in a recliner snoozing. Her mom was sitting on a sofa facing a TV set that was playing some sort of nature documentary.

"Ugh," Jenny whispered. "Another show about how dogs and cats became pets. Mom is like, totally obsessed. Look around though... no pets."

"What about your dog?" Jack asked.

"Dog? OH! Marty! Sorry, he's more like a brother or something to me at this point. I sometimes forget he's even here because he usually stays in his room downstairs."

"Your dog has its own room?"

"I think," I said, "that it would be easy to forget he's here right now... you know... because he isn't here."

"Oh!" Jenny said loud enough that her dad jumped out of his chair in a panic. "Sorry, Dad! Marty got out again! He bit Marsha!"

"What?" Jenny's mom said. "Red, go find him. We're lucky that child hasn't killed someone yet! Marsha, come on! Let's go get your bite treated!"

I was grabbed by my arm and basically thrown up a staircase at that point. Jenny was right; her mom was a little scary. She was tall, blonde, and looked a lot like what Jenny would look like if she were twenty years older and able to beat up King Kong. She wasn't physically scary; there was just something about the way she carried herself. I was reminded of watching shark videos with my dad. There was something going on behind her eyes. She knew she was the most dominant creature in any environment, but she chose not to annihilate everyone. It showed strength and restraint.

She never let go of my arm the whole way to the upstairs bathroom. She wasn't squeezing it, but I got the feeling that she had to make sure I was moving on her time and not my time. We passed a bedroom that had to be Jenny's; the door was open, and the floor was littered with open magazines ranging from fashion to monsters. Maybe the only time in my life I have seen a *Fangoria* sitting next to a *Delia*'s catalog. I had to fight off this weird, growing feeling of liking Jenny; that just wasn't what I needed right now at all.

"Jenny," her mom said. "Clean up your magazines."

She didn't yell; she just said it.

Jenny heard it though because I heard her feet running up the stairs. We passed a window, and I saw a car pulling out of the driveway, so Red listened too.

Oh yeah, Leslie Sirba was the alpha in this house. If she told me I had a nice dress, I would only buy that dress for the rest of my existence... probably after too. She was just... a force.

The bathroom was covered in lighthouses. Not sandy beach lighthouses like my grandma's house. There was something different about these. They looked haunted. There was something inside of them guiding ships to their ends instead of safety. I can't explain why that is; maybe it was that they were all dark and the pictures were at night, maybe it was the vibes that strangled some of them, maybe it was just that I was already scared of Leslie but wanted to blame it on haunted lighthouses or possessed dolls... anything but this woman who could snap me in two with a compliment.

She sat me down on a wooden bench by the bathtub. One thing I do want to be critical about; who has a bench in their bathroom? Just sit on the toilet lid like a normal person. She sat on the toilet lid... you know... like a normal person... and pulled my leg to her. I hadn't even told her where I was bitten, but she knew and was already cleaning the small mark with some sort of liquid and a sponge. She slapped a Band-Aid on it and pushed on my ankle for a minute.

"Sorry if it hurts," she said. "Pressure will help the magic little blood fairies... you're too old for that."

I smiled.

That was the mistake because that's when she popped the question.

"You must not like my daughter very much, do you?"

I didn't know what to say. I've already gone over all of this.

"It's okay," she said. "I'm not mad at you if you don't. Just... can you give it another try?"

She was vulnerable in that moment. The presence was gone; the fear was gone. She just wanted her daughter to be loved by this odd girl in her bathroom that she just put a Scooby-Doo band aid on.

"She's..." she took a deep breath. "She's... I think she can be overbearing to people at first. She worries about not fitting in. I think she overdoes it to force people to take her in. I get why someone as confident as you would see through that. For what it's worth, she loves you. She wishes she could be as calm, cool, and careless about what others think like you."

I'm not confident, I'm scared. Scared of what everyone will think of me if I say anything ever. Jenny not confident? Oh please. She's the most confident and loved person in our class. Parents don't know anything, do they?

After she got me taken care of, not that there was much to take care of, we made our way back down to the living room. Jack and Jenny were looking at magazines while the voice on the TV talked about how cats will sometimes bring their owners dead mice because they think they're bad hunters or something.

"Mom!" Jenny said. She held up this brochure like it was a trophy. "I was telling Jack about how we're going to camp in a couple weeks! He said he would go! Do you want to go too, Marsha?"

"Camp?" I asked. I said it like I didn't know what a camp was because saying, "so, I actually hate outdoors activities," probably wasn't going to go over so well right now.

"Yeah! Dad's been hired as camp counselor and mom is going to be the nurse! We're all going... except Marty... someone will have to babysit him."

I would say except Marty. I wouldn't take that dog to a camp unless I wanted it to be a new *Friday the 13th* movie.

"Oh," I said. "Why would I go? I mean... like not the way that sounded... what would be the purpose of me being there?"

"I don't know... I really wanted you and Jack to go. I don't know any of the other campers and having my best friends there would be great. You could also use it as a way to practice reporting something, maybe?"

Best friends?

She knew I wanted to be a reporter?

Was she insane?

Was this a camp for insane people?

I looked at Leslie. That was a mistake. She had this look in her eyes; this look that was basically pleading for me to try this for her daughter. I thought about how it must feel to be her, and how it must feel to be Jenny if her mom was right. Besides, if Jack was going, what else was I going to do all summer? I hate to admit it, but after seeing the vibes of her bedroom, I did sort of feel like I was being invited to a castle for dinner.

"Yeah, you know what? I would love to!"

And that was that.

Leslie put her hand on my shoulder and squeezed in a sort of thank you. Jack immediately started asking about boats. When did Jack start liking boats? Is this one of those weird things boys all want to talk about like that guy who jumped the Grand Canyon on his motorcycle?

I didn't want to go on a lake, but I guess I should have thought of that before I went off and became a camper at Camp Howling.

Chapter 3

Road Trip!

ONE THING YOU SHOULD know about me is that I hate being trapped in a car for a long time. It may be the sitting still while the world passes by at sixty miles an hour and not seeing any of it; or it may be feeling like I'm in a broom closet in the same sitting position for hours. One person can only fill out so many crosswords, finish so many word searches, and get annoyed trying to read comics while bouncing before they just take a nap. That's also the worst part; you wake up in a confusion because you fell asleep in Ohio and woke up in Boston. Maybe that's just me, but it's a little too close to teleportation for my comfort, and I have watched *The Fly*.

Riding in the Stirba's minivan was way different. Like not boring at all. Leslie and Red bickered in a lighthearted way about the directions, Jenny had figured out how to hook up a VCR so we could watch her Gamera movies (that yes, yes, I was quite jealous of), and they brought a cooler filled with soda. It was basically like hanging out in someone's bedroom. We decided on *Gamera vs. Gyaos*; it's the one with a giant vampire bat. There's this cool scene with... I don't know if you've watched it, so I won't spoil it. Just let me say this; it's a classic. Jenny knew all the lines, and I hate to admit it, but I was starting to see why Jack wanted to be around her so much.

Everything was going swimmingly. I wasn't even mad about being on the trip. I spent two weeks before we left dreading the trip; I asked my mom and dad to make up some kind of excuse to not let me go. They thought it would be good for my social life to get out of the house. Mom even bought me a new pair of pink cowboy boots to wear for confidence.

I did think this may be a good opportunity to really put my reporting dream to the test. I would be surrounded by strangers at camp, surely it would be easier to interview people when I knew I would probably never see them again in my life, right? What's the worst that can happen? I embarrass myself, have to deal with it for a few days, and then I forget about ever wanting to be a reporter and live up to my full potential as one of those weird mimes at the zoo or something. They don't still make silent movies, so acting was out of the question. Radio was definitely not an option at this point. I have a shyness that would be perfectly suited for working all night in a graveyard or something.

I'm terrified of zombies and ghosts though, so I'll probably skip that. Besides, graveyards aren't in need of a weird silent girl to... I actually don't know what jobs graveyards have to offer other than digging holes; I don't like doing that either.

Yeah, my mom and dad were no hope. They even came home from a night at the Stirba's in the best mood they've ever been in after meeting my friend's parents. When they met Jack's mom, they came home all sad that a single mom and her only child would watch *Wheel of Fortune* together every night. Personally, I think it's sweet that they do that, but my parents think *Wheel of Fortune* is the TV equivalent of the McRib sandwich. I do not have the time to elaborate on that, but they think it's a sign of complacency in life. I just think it's weird that it's a meat patty and it looks like plastic... but what do I know?

The two weeks went by in a heartbeat. I spent all of it trying to find a way to get out of this trip. I even faked sick a couple times but got caught eating a whole box of cereal one time and changing the tires on my bicycle another. I guess sick people don't get hungry or have ambition to fix a flat tire for when they are un-sick.

Well played, Mom and Dad, but I hope you miss me at least a little.

"Which exit was it?" Red asked. "I can't remember..."

"Red..." Leslie said closing her eyes. "You said you couldn't possibly forget the exit."

"What reason did I have?"

"That's what I asked."

"I'll not be stopping for directions."

"Yes, you will."

"Yeah, okay, I'll take the next exit."

What is it with dads and not asking for help on road trips? Is it really that hard to pull over and ask for help from someone who lives in the area and therefore knows the area a little better? My dad had driven us to Cleveland one time instead of pulling over and asking which exit would take us to Cincinnati. If you're not familiar with Ohio, those cities are at opposite ends of the state and my dad's understanding of how roads work is on opposite ends of the galaxy with how roads actually work.

We pulled into a gas station that looked like it teleported straight out of an '80s horror movie. I could almost hear an old person telling us we were doomed.

"Dad," Jenny said. "This looks... I don't know... somewhat abandoned."

"It's fine," Red said. "Come in with me and get some drinks and snacks on me."

"Who else would be buying them? None of us have jobs."

We got out of the van and Jack decided that was the perfect time to lay belly down on the ground and kiss the dirt-covered asphalt. He's never once told me he hates being in cars, so this was a new development for me.

"That van," Jack said, standing up. "It felt like I was in a spaceship, so I thought I'd tell Earth I missed it."

Jenny rolled her eyes and went into the station. I paused and tapped Jack on the shoulder and pointed toward a sign on the road. It was a billboard that read "Camp Howling five miles ahead!"

"Yeah," Jack said. "Guess Red will be laughed at in there. Either way, I hope they have grape soda."

There were little bells over the door that jingled when we opened it. Red and the worker paused mid conversation to look at us. The worker looked just like you would expect a worker in a gas station from a horror movie would look. He had a ball cap, overalls, and a calico cat on the counter. He was telling Red that he should rethink the job; apparently the camp has a lot of maintenance problems and it's really just a big headache. Every point he made, the cat would look at him, then at Red, and then let out a long meow that sounded a lot like, "tell them nothing more," to me. Cats are weird like that.

I browsed the aisles and decided a bag of potato chips that expired two months ago last year wasn't what I was craving and settled for a cream soda. It was called Gem and looked like liquid gold. I tried it when we got back to the van, and I will confirm it is liquid gold.

The conversation about the maintenance issues had reached the point that Red was being told about a cabin with a missing back door that would probably be the home to a million little critters by now. Red seemed to think it wouldn't be an issue; the worker said it would be.

Leslie walked in front of me with Jenny beside her; Jack followed behind. They set drinks and snacks on the counter and Leslie interrupted the conversation.

"I really think we can probably just not use that one cabin," she said. "The critters will be happy, we'll be happy, it will be all groovy."

She turned to me and winked as she took the Gem.

"I don't know what it is with guys," she said handing the worker cash. "You would argue over who was holding a greener blade of grass before admitting you were wrong. Keep the change. Red, there's a sign outside that says the camp is five miles away."

"Oh," Red said. "Did you get me anything?"

"RC Cola."

"Oh, okay… well… I guess I'll be seeing you later?"

Red followed Leslie out the door with Jack and Jenny behind them. When I made it to the door, I heard the old man's voice.

"Hey, kid," he said to me. I turned and looked at him. "Please. Do whatever you can. Don't go to that camp. It's bad news. People don't come back."

Of course I would be the one to get the weird speech. I left in a hurry and hopped in the van without mentioning it. Leslie was right, men would do anything to avoid admitting they're wrong. This guy probably convinced himself there was a masked killer at the camp and that's why he didn't see the people again. It couldn't be on account of him having Zebra Cakes that expired a year ago; no, never.

"Look what I found!" Jack said. He was holding a plastic bottle of Crystal Pepsi and his smile was so big and round that Tony Hawk would win a contest skating it. As long as I can remember, Jack has complained that Crystal Pepsi was gone. It was his favorite drink. "Oh, wait… best by May 1995… oh well… not the best is still better than nothing!"

Maybe the guy was right, maybe people really didn't make it back.

Chapter 4

Camp Tummy Ache

JACK IS THE ONLY person I know who can eat a large pizza, an entire order of breadsticks, a box of Star Crunch for dessert, and wash it down with two jugs of soda without feeling sick. You think that's an exaggeration but ask his mom about why she doesn't like taking him out to eat, and she'll tell you about the time he ordered four Double Whoppers at Burger King, and she had to take a loan from the bank to buy it. He eats and eats but his body never grows. He's always just looked like... Jack.

You could put him in a lineup of other teenage boys and probably not be able to pick him out. He's even got the same Charlotte Hornets jacket every boy our age has for some reason. None of them like the Hornets, and I know for a fact that Jack doesn't even like basketball. Besides, if he were a basketball fan, he would probably like the Denver Nuggets on account of the name reminding him of food, and his favorite NFL team is the

Broncos. I have no idea why he chose a team from Colorado named after a horse, but here we are. That's just life with Jack.

With all of this information, it should come as no surprise that when we made it to the camp, the first place Jack wanted to find was the kitchen. Red told us where it was and made us promise to not eat anything out of date. I made that promise immediately; I was never at risk of doing it. Jenny was complaining about stomach pains, and I was starting to get them too. I didn't even eat any of the gas station stuff, so just being in proximity to it must have been enough. I picture years-expired seasonings flying from potato chips like jet fighters and going into the pores on my body. That's how dastardly that food had to be.

The camp was laid out in a half circle around a lake; around ten cabins formed in a "U." A road went around them in a loop, with a smaller one going between them and splitting the number in half. We pulled in behind a row of cabins, but between them you could see a hill leading downward to the water. The water was that weird greenish-blue color that you will end up calling blue, but one of your friends will argue it's actually green. One of those things where you spend more time arguing over the beautiful thing than just enjoying the beautiful thing. We found a path behind the cabins and started exploring. I think Jenny and I had some sort of telepathic link through a shared stomachache because we both knew exactly where he was going without speaking about it.

"Jack," Jenny said as we struggled to keep up with him. "Jack, I don't want to go see more food. I'm going to barf."

"Yeah, Jack," I said. "I don't feel so hot either."

"Come on," Jack said. "I just want to see what they have. Sheesh, what happened to girl power and all of that?"

Jenny picked up a pinecone and tossed it at Jack's head. He ducked it effortlessly. It was a bad throw. "Oh," Jack said. "Too sick to go with me, but just fine enough to try and assassinate me!"

"That's..." Jenny said. "That's not the right word."

"Yeah, it is. If you would stay awake during Mr. Z's vocab reviews, you'd know that assassinate means to kill someone important to society."

"That's where the word is wrong."

"I'm a pretty important guy. Why else am I here?"

"No... the part about killing. If I were trying to kill you... you'd be dead."

Jenny brushed past Jack looking more annoyed than I had ever seen her.

"Hey!" Jack said. He punched me on the arm and pointed to Jenny who was currently storming off in epic fashion. "She said I was important... you know... in a roundabout way... I'll take it!"

If there's one thing Jack likes more than food, it's compliments. He can twist an insult about a bad hair cut into a compliment about his facial structure. "No," he would say, "my face is just so perfectly shaped that a standard haircut from a standard barber in a standard establishment such as this can't do it justice."

Meanwhile, I'll find a way to make a compliment into something somehow being a mistake or a social faux pas I've somehow committed. Oh, you like my outfit? That must mean you're saying it's unique, that must mean that you think it's different in a bad way, that must mean that better judgement has fled my mind again, and I am the worst person on Earth to go shopping with. I'm telling you; I could find a way to feel like I owe someone an apology for giving them my lunch on stuffed-crust pizza Friday.

Something was ferociously wrong with my stomach. I was a little jealous that Jenny had complimented Jack. It wasn't even really a compliment. I think she was going for more of an "action movie bad-ass" line and adding something about him being an annoying boy who has been known to eat a booger in the past would have ruined the flow. Still, something was different with me. Jenny wasn't getting on my nerves nearly as bad. I chalked it up to being sick and having a healthy fear of Mrs. Stirba.

The kitchen wasn't too far off; just down a little dusty path. The path went through a small patch of dense wooded area and then opened up into a circular-shaped yard with picnic tables, benches, and a fire pit outside of what had to be some sort of a community building or meeting place for the camp.

We approached it from the back, walking up a slight hill. It was a long building with one single floor. The front side had a porch with a swing set. We walked up the six stairs and noticed Jenny looking past us at the scenery. Jack and I both decided to humor her and turned around as well.

It was gorgeous. I can't even begin to lie about that. From the porch, the view was of the lake. Green trees lined the shores; it looked more like a movie set than a real place. A few boat docks and little sheds were on the shore behind the row of cabins. The cabins were aligned so that their front porches and doorways were facing out toward the lake. It really was the kind of thing you would see in a movie or TV show about some kids at camp. I was hoping this was more the kind with fun but harmless pranks, and not the kind where some old janitor who got burned up like a Big Mac back in 1972 decided that this was the year to exact revenge on the campers. I'd rather see Jack's underwear hanging from the flagpole than his head.

I made a mental note to not go on any rafting trips.

"Hey!" Jenny yelled while cupping her hands around her mouth to form a funnel for the sound. "We found the kitchen!"

I scanned the shoreline and found Red and Leslie checking over a boat. Red was kneeling and looking at something while Leslie took notes. They looked at us, and both gave us a thumbs up.

"Jenny!" Red yelled. He cupped his mouth in the same way. Like father like daughter, I guess. "It's going to be getting dark here soon, find some food we can cook on a fire and head back, okay?"

"Yeah, Dad! That's fine!"

"Hey, Mr. Stirba!" Jack yelled. He tried to mimic the face-cup method but ended up putting a slight mute on his voice. "Why don't you catch us something out of the lake!"

"That's because the only time I like seafood is when I see food and I eat it!"

I felt the Earth's rotation go off course as Jenny, Jack, Leslie, and myself all rolled our eyes at the same time. The cringe was so bad that our subsequent eyeroll had to create a dynamic change in the earth's axis. In thirty years, they would call this moment, "The Dad Joke That Ruined the World." I hope George Miller directs it.

The door was swinging shut behind Jack, who apparently could no longer stand waiting on us to go in. He said his piece and decided it was expired food time. We followed a little more patiently.

"I need to sit down," Jenny said. "My stomach is killing me."

I couldn't disagree with her; my stomach was in knots. I was right about the building being some sort of community building. There was a small stage at one end, long tables that you would see in our school's cafeteria, and a podium off to the side for speeches. Banners hung everywhere declaring what canoeing contests were held here and what schools won them. I couldn't find Colony High anywhere; which I would be a little more bummed about if our school actually had a canoeing team.

I heard doors opening and closing on the opposite end of the room. Had to be Jack in the kitchen. Sure enough, I heard him mumbling about if it would be good to cook cheesesteak over a campfire. He quickly realized that he couldn't do that with a stick, but maybe he would take a pan.

I stood up and walked to a window at the back of the building. I could see the lake and cabins still. But I could also see another building off in the distance on a hill. There were some archery stations set up between the cabins and the building as well. The building itself looked sort of creepy. Think of an abandoned castle in the middle of a dark and stormy night and you'd have the right image in your head, only make the castle a cabin with two floors and a wraparound porch.

"Hey, Jenny," I said. "What's with the creepy mansion cabin over there?"

"That's where we're going to stay," Jenny said. She stood up and walked over to me. "See, there goes Mom and Dad."

Red and Leslie were both loaded down with book bags and walking up the hill like soldiers carrying an entire troops' inventory. They had all of our stuff between the two of them.

"Sheesh," I said. "That has to be a lot of weight. They don't even look bothered."

"Dad is still on the force in his mind, so he works out all of the time, and Mom is... well... you've met her."

I bobbled my head around. Yeah, Leslie being super strong made sense. She could probably carry all of those bags and Red without breaking a sweat. She could probably tell them all to float, and they would instantly defy gravity.

Jack came out of the kitchen with a plastic bag filled with food, another with cans of soda, and a third with some cooking utensils. "I'm going to show you guys how to cook," he said while pointing a spatula at the ceiling. He looked like a barbarian wielding the sword he spent seven days questing for. Sometimes I wonder if Jack actually wants to be my friend, or if he just likes my mom's cooking and cooking lessons; but then I remember he didn't know what my mom did for work until he had already decided I was his best friend. That's actually how he found out. He said that best friends should go to each other's houses and meet each other's families instead of just parting ways on the walk home from school. Really, I just think he wasn't done talking to me and decided to follow me home like some sad, lost, and chatty puppy. I've been stuck with him ever since; at least the whole feast of boogers thing came to an end.

"Oh, wow," Jack said. "Look how fast it's getting dark! We don't have a flashlight or anything. We better go!"

I looked out the window. It was just daylight a few minutes ago; but Jack was right; it was already starting to look dark outside. It happened so fast that I could almost hear my dad saying, "it gets dark so fast now," in my mind.

Have you ever watched one of those movies where people move into a house and don't notice a strange door until it's too late? I always thought those movies were dumb, most people search their new home from top to bottom for ghosts before moving in, right? Or did my parents just tell me they did that so I wouldn't feel scared all the time?

You know what?

Don't answer that.

The point is that we had overlooked a door, and that door was now bowing outward from whatever was bashing against it from the other side. In our defense, it was a small door. It was really more of a half door laid on its side. It was under the stage, off to the right. There was a chain and padlock keeping it closed, but the hinges were starting to buckle from the strength of the blows.

"That's probably a deer," Jenny said.

Whatever it was, I didn't want to hear Jenny's misidentification. Neither did the misidentified deer because it let out a roar at the sound of her voice. It sounded like Jenny's dog, Marty, but way lower and way meaner.

"I think if deer made those noises," Jack said backing up to the front entrance, "they would probably be hunting us instead."

Another loud blow hit the door and one of the hinges flew across the building. Four fingers slid out from the new opening. The fingers were long, covered in brown fur, and ended in the longest nails I have ever seen.

"Okay," Jenny said, "that may be Bigfoot."

She grabbed my arm, and we started running. We leaped down the front stairs and rolled across the ground from the impact. When we stood up and started moving again, we heard the wood from inside shattering as another one of those awful roars chased us like it had a physical presence. I didn't stop to look back; we were already into a patch of woods and running downhill toward the lake and cabins.

Another explosion of wood and a roar filled the night sky followed by branches being broken from behind us.

We made it to the shore and started running for a cabin.

"In here!" Jack whispered. He was under an upside-down boat holding a finger over his mouth so we would be quiet. Another roar followed us down the hill, and I didn't have time to wonder if getting under a boat would be helpful or not. It would just have to work.

We hid for what felt like forever listening to whatever that thing was stomping around, sniffing, and letting out those roars. The mud around the boat squished inside our hideout from the thing walking so close. We kept hearing a noise that had to be the thing dragging its nails across the wood above our heads.

The sound of a nose working overtime was right outside of our hideaway. The thing climbed on top of the boat, it sunk into the mud and sand forcing us to get closer to each other. We would be trapped if it sunk too far. Something about science and pressure that I didn't pay attention to enough to describe but know is very much a thing and at that time, was a very real fear. We heard the howl that Cerberus would let out if he were real from above us and then the sounds of water splashing as the thing ran off down shore in search of what I could only guess were more kids to torture. Sheesh, go to a mouse's pizza place or anywhere else but here.

Jenny pointed toward the cabins, I nodded, Jack shook his head. Jenny made a motion that showed how two people out-voted one, and we lifted the boat from our heads.

You would think that having already committed one bad idea from a horror movie, we wouldn't do it a second time... you would also think that then we would know enough to not do it a third time...

Sadly, you would be wrong.

Chapter 5

Invisible Doorways

THE BOAT FLIPPING OVER to be water ready must have flipped a switch somewhere out in the cosmos because as soon as it hit the ground, the growling started. Whatever it was, it had decided that running through mud actually made it scarier; I'm always one to appreciate a little bit of atmosphere, but this felt excessive. We were already scared; we didn't need to hear it slogging through mud. The splash, smoosh, pop of four huge legs going into the mud and pulling back out with little to no chances of slowing down just made me worry more about the strength of our pursuer.

A small voice inside of me wondered if maybe we were over-reacting here; what if it didn't want to hurt us, but just wanted to hang out? I'm not one to judge, but if running across a lake shore makes you sound like a monster truck with a deep enough growl that you could be in a death metal band, I'm going to run from you even if you have my mom's Hawaiian pizza and a check for two billion bucks. It's probably a personal problem, but I'll work on it later... I promise.

We made it up the hill without anyone slipping and falling back down. I was surprised about that and still am; here we are, being the worst horror movie characters of all time, and we still managed to not fall. But I guess that made us worse? A good character always falls; they're usually the ones that survive. We were in the cabin with the door shut long before the beast of Howling Lake collided with the wood and sent a crack through it.

This door had the same issue as the one at the community building; the hinges were not strong. Couldn't they go to the gym? Jenny and I started grabbing things to sit in front of it.

"Hey, guys," Jack said.

"Not now, Jack," I said.

"No, I really think—"

"NOT NOW!" Jenny and I both screamed at him as we turned to see what he was yammering on about. He stood in a different room that was only separated by a bit of bordering wood forming a sort of square archway. He pointed to a wide-open door behind him and shrugged.

"That man did tell your dad about that," I said.

"What do I look like?" Jenny said. "The Map Maker of Howling Lake? I've never even been here before!"

Jack put his finger to his lips and told us to quiet down. We both walked into the room he was in. I was thinking of making a run for it up until I heard something heavy walking on the roof. Each step filled me more and more with dread. It wasn't old Saint Nick up there. I knew that because it was summer, and there wasn't a chimney in here that I could see.

"Hey," Jenny whispered from inside the chimney I didn't notice. Still, I know it wasn't Santa. She waved us toward her, and we walked as slowly as we could. When I look back, that was kind of silly, right? Whatever was on the roof knew we were in that cabin; why would it matter if we were quiet or not?

The chimney was a bit of a hidden doorway. It looked like the back had been carved out to connect to a walk-in closet behind. The closet was covered in plywood to block any other entryway into the secret room. A sleeping bag lay on the floor to the left, and a stack of books was on the right. It was still light enough outside that we could see just good enough to make out claw marks all over the inside of the wall.

"Do you think…" Jack started. "That someone caught a bear in here?"

"Why would someone do that?" Jenny asked.

"For science?"

"Science? How?"

"I don't know… to observe how a bear would live in a walk-in closet?"

"Oh," I said, "I guess bears love reading books about lycanthropy too, huh?"

"Like a trophy?"

"Lycanthropy…"

"Werewolves," Jenny said. "Lycanthropy is werewolves. I think."

"You think?" Jack asked.

Jenny just shrugged and held up two books.

So, You've Been Bitten by a Werewolf: What Now?

How to Make Friends as a Werewolf.

"This guy," Jack said. "At least he's taking a progressive approach to the whole thing."

"And," Jenny said, "he has a low self-image problem."

"Relatable," I said.

Jenny and Jack just nodded along.

A loud thud hit the ground outside somewhere. I could guess it was where the missing door was because I'm not an idiot; where else would the werewolf land?

"What if he's a she?" Jack asked.

"Huh?" Jenny asked.

"We think it's a guy with low self-worth, what if it's a woman."

"Jack," Jenny said, cupping her face into her hands. "Please shut up."

Jack made a zipper motion across his mouth followed by a locking motion and then threw away his imaginary key.

Footsteps sounded out on the wood flooring. The boards groaned under the weight of the intruder. It let out a guttural roar and stomped past the chimney entrance into the first room. We could hear it sniffing around and moving the things we piled in front of the door. Something would slam against the wall, and we would jump. Another piece of something would slide across the floor in front of us. Finally, it let out another gurgle and moved quickly to the chimney.

It was dark enough outside at this point that I could only make out an outline and some details of its face. The important parts I noticed were the long nails, the razor-sharp teeth inside of its snout, and bright green eyes that were filled with hunger.

The werewolf couldn't fit into the chimney entrance; its frame was too big. It laid on its belly and clawed inside with one hand trying to reach us. It put its arm in as deep as possible before making some movements with its body; the sound of bones crunching and muscle stretching was almost as bad as the roaring. It got closer this time, but still not close enough. Its five claws digging deep into the wood and creating grooves as it slowly pulled its hand back.

When it pulled back out, it stood up to full height on two legs. We heard the crunching of bones again; apparently putting its shoulder back in place. It growled and ran around the rooms hitting the walls and digging into others with its nails.

"I think we're safe in here," Jack said.

"For now," Jenny said. "Let's hope this isn't the person who sleeps in here. They may know a different way in if it is."

That was a scary thought.

If that were possible, we may not have long before the vague memory of what happens when its human kicks in.

"Look at this," Jenny said holding up a book. "Diary of Ted Brett - A Werewolf."

"Not the best title," Jack said. "It's a little bit too on the nose."

"Literary criticism aside, he definitely lives here."

We all involuntarily turned to look at the plywood covering the door.

"Let's hope it swings inwards then," I said.

"'Day one,'" Jenny read in a whisper. She had to position herself just right to read. The room was too dark to see the words at this point, but if she angled herself just right, the moonlight shone through a gash in the ceiling. "'I treated the wound. I used everything I could find in the nurse's station. Still, nothing doing. It continues to grow hair. It's strange... the spot where I was bitten is totally healed... but hair sprouts from the circular bite mark in heavy tufts. I'm very lucky it's on my upper arm or that would be hard to hide, and I don't have enough lies to explain it away when people ask at the store.'"

"Wow," Jack said. "He definitely has a self-worth issue."

The noise outside had stopped. I got the feeling that he had gone away after realizing he couldn't reach us.

"Why else would he be worried about that?" Jack said.

Jenny shook her head and continued reading.

"'I first noticed a few weeks after my bite. It wasn't a full moon, just night in general. As soon as the sun would set... I could feel myself changing. Almost as if the sunlight was keeping the wolf at bay, instead of the full moon forcing the change.'"

Jenny shook her head. "Weird," she said. "'I thought… okay, so movie stuff is never right. Anyway… The change came on all at once the first night. I couldn't control it at all. The sun would set just enough, and my body began to crackle like cooking popcorn. The bones rearranged, my skin stretched… I felt miserable. I'm still myself in there… just really mad. I feel like everyone, and everything is my worst enemy when the change hits.'"

A loud pounding hit the wall followed by clawing. Jack held up a small frying pan and prepared for war.

"Jack," I said. "You couldn't leave that stuff?"

"It was wrapped around my arm!"

We heard pieces of wood hitting the ground in the room behind us. Then, heavy footfalls made their way to the door. We heard it open—no luck for me, it opened outwards—and the thudding and clawing started on the makeshift wall between us and thousands of pounds of sharp death-inducing teeth and nails. The board pushed back at the top, and the snout poked through. It opened and slammed shut rapidly. I think it was trying to scare us out of the room instead of breaking in.

Jack hit the wall with the pan and the wolf cried out in pain. It let out a growl and slammed into the wall.

"Jack!" Jenny yelled. "Try and throw the food out there!"

Jack ripped open bags of bread, meat, cheese, and seasonings and dumped them through the gap the wolf's snout created. We heard it chomping away and swallowing everything. Hopefully some of it was expired and he would be as sick as I was.

"Now," I whispered and crawled as fast as I could out of the room.

We hurried through the cabin and ran out the door we had blocked. Everything was moved now, but the noise the thing was making would cover our exit sounds. It would probably be trying to get into that room for hours.

Jenny started to scream when she opened the door. A figure was standing there holding a weapon that looked like a rifle.

Red covered her mouth and picked her up. He motioned us out of the back door and then he shut it. He ran with his head lowered to the ground. When we passed a window, I could see the wolf inside thrashing against the wall still trying to get in. Red stayed hunched over all the way back to the big cabin on the hill.

When we got inside, he shut the door and locked too many dead bolts to count.

"We told you to come back before dark," Leslie said. "Now you'll have the local werewolf all worked up for the night."

Chapter 6

The Local What?

ONE REASON I KNOW I will be a good full time news reporter is that I can pick up on little hints and gain a lot of ground on a story from those hints. For example, I know my mom is making apple pie because she's cutting up apples while a pie crust is in a pan waiting for filling. Another example would be that I can always tell my dad is about to go on a rant about something that annoys him because he will say, "you know what really annoys me?" and then starts yammering. Or, just another wild example of how I can see a huge story in a teeny tiny eenie weenie little hint: when someone refers to a local werewolf as a local werewolf, I have to take a big step on a tiny limb and assume they know more about the werewolf in question than I do.

Leslie calling the werewolf a local told me two things: one, that she knew there was a werewolf before we ever got here; and two, my least favorite revelation, the gas station creep was right.

People probably didn't return from here often and unfortunately it was because they were probably no longer among the living. A quick side note, can werewolves get sick from eating humans that have gone past a certain date? Like, am I going to make him sick in like five years? I think that's a good goal to set for myself, be the type of girl who makes a werewolf sick after it eats you.

The cabin wasn't making me sick though. It had one of those cool overhanging balconies and about six rooms on each floor. That's as many doors as I counted before Leslie hit us with the local werewolf thing.

"Okay," Jenny said, lifting her hands in the air. "I haven't been fully honest."

"Oh, boy," Red said. Leslie pulled him over to a sofa, and they both sat there leaving it all up to their teenage daughter to tell us the truth.

"Remember Marty?" Jenny asked.

"Your freaked out dog?" Jack said.

"How could I forget?" I said.

"Well," Jenny said. "Marty isn't a dog. I mean not in the traditional sense. He's a canine, totally a canine... are wolves canines? Are werewolves canines? Mom?"

"Keep going, honey," Leslie said from the couch. "You're doing great."

"Marty is my older brother."

Jenny winced when she said it. I think she believed our words would shoot out like barbs and attach to her. I guess if I had brought Jack and Jenny to an abandoned camp that was the home to a werewolf, I would think I was going to be hit too. I would also never do that because I don't particularly care to know where any werewolves live. Kind of an "I can't see them; they can't see me" sort of thing.

"Marty was bitten around two months ago," Jenny said. "He was taking mom dinner at the hospital. When he got there, he spotted an ambulance with the back door open. Nothing too unusual, but it had driven over a curb and crashed into a tree. Marty was going to the academy in the fall, so he was already planning to follow Dad's footsteps. Dad had already been hurt, so he took it more seriously. Anyway, he was checking it out when this... thing... pulled Marty into the bushes and bit him. It would have killed him but someone inside the ambulance shot a flare at it. They didn't know what happened; they went and got a sick man who then turned into a monster right in front of them."

"Yeah," Jack said. "Totally plausible. Sounds just like the start of a horror movie. Let me guess, you three decided to follow the werewolf that bit Marty here and destroy it?"

"Wrong," Leslie said. She stood up and went to the next room. We all let her have her dramatic effect. She came back with a can of soda. "We got a note from the werewolf, Ted Brett, telling us to come here. He said he had found a way to trap himself as the wolf. I can see now that he had no idea what he was talking about and now I know why Marty keeps getting out."

"Speaking of," I said. "Where is he? Is he just at home with some poor babysitter? Is he in a doggy vacation home? Where is the other werewolf?"

"He's here," Red said. "He's in one of the other cabins. He's been sedated for the night. Ted has been trying to teach him how to control the change so that it doesn't happen every night. But, from what little knowledge I have, it looks like Marty's state has made Ted regress and change nightly instead."

Red walked around with his finger at his mouth. Very modern thinking man.

"Oh," I said, "that's great news! Two werewolves for the price of one! Why did you make me and Jack come along on this weird little get together? How do you know there are two? Don't they look the same? Maybe that was Marty?"

"I was scared," Jenny said. "I thought having you here would give you a huge story to report on. You could get on NBC or CBS with a real-life werewolf story. They both have gray fur, sure. Marty has a white patch on his chest... and besides, it's the same as telling two pugs apart... I know that wasn't Marty. Jack... well... sorry, Jack. I just knew there was no way Marsha would be here without you."

"That's okay," Jack said. "If my best friend, and the girl I have a crush on... I mean... no... well... sorry... if you're both getting eaten by a werewolf, I guess I would want to be here to help you."

"We know he likes meat," I said with an eyeroll. "He was distracted by the cheesesteak stuff."

"Cheesesteak?" Red asked. He looked toward us with a hopeful gaze. "That's my favorite."

"Tough luck, Dad," Jenny said. "If you had made sure Ted was locked up like he said he was, you'd be eating cheesesteak right now. Jack probably learned how to make it from Marsha's mom. She's a real-life chef!"

"I had cheese whiz and everything, Mr. Stirba," Jack said.

Red snapped his fingers one time in frustration. Leslie shooshed him. "The good news," Leslie said. "Is we're only going to have to make it until the morning. Then we can just get Marty and leave."

"Why don't you leave Marty here?" I asked. "He may be better off with this other guy."

"No, I want my son to be my son again. I'll do whatever it takes."

There it was. That same look she gave me that convinced me to come along on this dumb trip in the first place. Camp counselors my big toe! These people were nutters!

"When is sunrise?" Jack asked.

"About six or seven in the morning," Red said.

"What time is it now?"

"Nine."

"Swell."

"Apparently, it's the strongest at midnight too. As in, that's when the werewolf is fully formed."

"Cool," I said. "I need to lay down."

My stomach was absolutely killing me. I felt like my insides were trying to force their way out of my rib cage. It was like a cramp in your leg, but at all times.

"I do too," Jenny said. "I feel like garbage."

"Look at this," Leslie said holding the open book. "It's his journal! It says, 'this is terrible. I think I ate a deer last night. I need help. I'm going to call nine-one-one and see if they can do anything about it.' That has to be when he came to the hospital."

"What do the first few pages say?" I asked. If I was going to make a story out of this, I needed all the info I could get."

"'Day one.'"

"We already read that. Weird hair growth. Maybe he should sell out to Rogaine."

"Hmmm, this is weird. 'When I woke up this morning, I was back at the camp. I felt at home. It must have something to do with being bitten here when I was hiking. I don't know where that wolf went as I can find no sign of him or her around. This is the place that news lady went missing at for a day or two a few years back. She said she just got mixed up after reporting on the camp's big canoe race and staying for a night hike. She couldn't have been gone more than a day because the news didn't cover it too long—that's irrelevant.'"

"Not to me it isn't," I said. I knew where we were now. When Anne Ambrose went missing three years ago, everyone assumed it was a kidnapping. The news broke after she was gone one whole day and night. It wasn't that big of a deal because she came stumbling back into camp the next morning saying she just got separated from the group on a night hike. It wasn't a big deal; she slept by the lake and followed it back. I never could remember the name of the camp, but I do remember how it was shut down before summer ended. Apparently, parents didn't like it when the reporter who was sent to cover the first race got lost at the place where their kids were supposed to spend a whole summer. I couldn't blame them; seems like the kind of thing you would make sure didn't happen if you didn't want parents thinking your camp was a death trap.

I absolutely did research about it. There wasn't really much to it sadly. She said she was walking, saw something move in the distance that distracted her just long enough for her group to move on and lose her. It doesn't make a lot of sense, does it? You would have to be extremely distracted for that to happen. My long-running theory was that something had captured her and held her hostage until she broke free. My second theory was that she found Bigfoot and had to convince them that she wouldn't tell anyone about them. Anne would have understood the massive ramifications of telling the general public that Bigfoot was real... Okay, maybe that would be my numero uno theory... not after the whole werewolf thing though; It was werewolves after that. Of course she didn't tell anyone that; they would have laughed her off the face of the Earth. Still, I didn't have the time or patience to take everyone down that particular rabbit hole.

"It shut down," I told everyone. "Anne Ambrose got lost here. Nothing bad. Just a night and a half or something. But the parents freaked out and made all the kids go home."

"Yeah," Leslie said. "I get that. I can also see how this place would be perfect for a werewolf. No one lives even close to here; that gas station was at least five miles back. They could survive during the day just fine and then run the woods at night."

"Want to know an eerie thought I just had?" Jack asked. "I bet he called the ambulance from that gas station. How far was the hospital you worked at from here?"

"I would say a twenty-minute drive from there," Leslie said. "I bet that's exactly what happened. He walked to the station and ran out of time."

"I need to lay down," Jenny said. She immediately laid on the floor. It was like all of the energy drained from her body. Red picked her up and carried her up the stairs into a room.

"I could use some rest too," I said. "My head feels like it's growing into a planet of its own. My stomach hurts. And my leg feels like it's out of place and bent around all weird."

"Good idea," Red said. "You all get some rest; I'll stand guard for a bit."

Leslie showed us to our rooms on the second floor. Jack's was a little smaller than mine, so I took that as a win for me. Mine had a queen-sized bed, a closet, and a window facing outside. There was a large cabinet too, but Leslie took it upon herself to move it in front of the window, so I didn't have to worry about a werewolf peeking or jumping in. I was pretty high up, but stranger things have happened today; Jack gave away food.

"Hey," Leslie said, sitting down on the bed beside me. "I'm sorry it's all gone badly, but I'm happy you're giving Jenny another chance."

"I don't know what good that does," I said. "She convinced you to let her bring me and my best friend to a camp to be eaten by a werewolf. Not the best move to win someone over. Actually, on my list of best moves, it falls just below spraying me with whatever the Loch Ness Monster eats and putting me on a plane to Scotland."

"Yeah, you're right. Sorry."

Leslie had perfected this whole sad-mother-wants-daughter-to-have-a-friend act on me, and I fell right for it again.

"Leslie," I said. She paused and turned to me at the doorway. "It's okay. Your family is worried about Marty. Jenny wasn't thinking clearly. I think I can sort of get it. It will be fine. We can trauma bond in the morning. You're a good mom."

Leslie nodded at me; a single tear ran down her cheek.

When she closed the door, I let out the biggest sigh I could and kicked my legs back and forth. This was crazy! Of all the ways to meet people and become a reporter, this was never one I had in my barrel of ideas.

I sat up after my tiny temper tantrum and started taking off my shoes. When I took off my shoe, I noticed a few long hairs growing from around my sock. When I took the sock off, I could see I had a bigger problem than the werewolf outside.

The spot that Marty had bitten me was covered in long, thick, brown hair.

Chapter 7

I Always Feel Like Somebody's Watching Me

I HAVE NEVER LOOKED into if a werewolf has x-ray vision or not; I'm nearly positive they do not. I don't think a creature with super speed, strength, and senses should also be able to see through a wall. I have to be honest, knowing that there was one out there right then, and knowing how terrifyingly fast it was; I think with the ability to see through walls, it would be an unstoppable predator, and humans would cease to exist. They could probably start farming us and making money. Werewolf capitalism. Good band name. Fantastic band name.

Either way, the scratching and clawing I heard outside my window that night had me convinced. I had never thought of it as a thing until then. I had to stop staring at that long hair on my ankle for a little bit, so that was good. It had all but made me freeze in place.

What would become of me? Would I ever be able to go back to school? Would I be stuck out here with two boys I've never met when they weren't salivating animals? Is that any different than any of the other boys I know?

What about my future? I couldn't be the world's first werewolf reporter, could I? I could not understand any words from the growling earlier; no one would watch that show. Maybe I could start an all-werewolf news all the time type of thing? A special channel? There has to be a market for the werewolf versions of the NFL or NBA. I could be the one to bring that to the masses. The only real problem there is I have only met two werewolves and both of them were trying to eat me. Unless werewolves can understand each other somehow, payment negotiations were going to be tough.

My brain was racing like that. I have never really been what you would call focused; my mind tends to wander off and think of weird scenarios. Yeah, just like the werewolf NBA; although if there is basketball in *Teen Wolf*, maybe it isn't too far-fetched. Bad choice of words there because then I started wondering if werewolves played fetch. I didn't want to be in some weird game of chase the stick that some weirdo has thrown for the rest of my life. Werewolves are immortal too, that's what I remembered; would I be stuck playing fetch for a thousand years?

I shook these thoughts from my head and stood up from the bed. My stomach immediately felt like I had been punched. I had to sit down quickly because I felt like I was going to puke if I took a few more steps. The scratching was getting louder. It was driving me insane. I wanted to hide, but I also had to see what was scratching. It was a double standard I was not ready to drill my brain about.

I took it slowly and managed to get moving toward the dresser. When I put my ear close to it, I noticed the clawing was a little distant sounding. It wasn't right at my window, but maybe below. I pulled the dresser back from the window as softly as I could, which turned out to not be softly at all. It slid across the floor with ease; so much ease that I was terrified it would burst through a wall.

I cupped my hands around my face to look out the window and saw nothing. As an experiment, I moved my hands. I could see outside into the dark just as well. Great, I was totally turning into a werewolf.

I sniffed at the air and my nose locked in on something off to the right. I tilted my head slightly to see the side of the house. I saw something moving and the scratching got louder. It smelled like old food and grass. I focused my eyes on the movement and realized it was a raccoon. The scratching was coming from the little thing's tiny claws against the wooden sides of a box to store trash bags in. The raccoon had opened a couple bags that had to be months old at this point and rummaged for food. I assumed this was Ted's trash place and felt fear because that means he would know his way around this cabin too.

I was fascinated with the raccoon; it was just using those tiny little claws to get more old food into its mouth. I couldn't believe how clearly I could see it, how well I could smell it.

Both the raccoon and I heard a noise in the woods. It was clawing, but from much bigger claws. The raccoon looked up toward me. We made eye contact, and I swear I could hear it thinking about how we both needed to hide from whatever was making that noise.

A white blur moved through the trees. That was enough for me to hide. I ran and jumped into the bed, pulling the covers over my face. As I'm sure you have learned by now, I'm a firm believer in the "if you can't see it, it can't see you" method of hiding. It's a flawed thought process. Especially when you consider that just a few seconds before, I was listening to a raccoon thirty feet away and through a wall as it clawed at wood. The werewolf would surely see me as a lump in a bed and smell me. My only hope was that it wouldn't climb the wall to look in the window.

That hope was crushed a few minutes later when I heard heavy breathing against the window. I peeked out from the covers, and the window was totally blacked out. It just looked like a regular window at night; I assumed it was dark because my heightened senses had vanished in fear in the same way I wanted too. They probably ran off with the small animal. That raccoon probably had super smelling at that point.

I got up, somehow finding the courage, and went to the window. I cupped my hands around my face again and could see nothing. The super sight was definitely gone. I breathed a sigh of relief. The warm air from my mouth made a line of fog above my head... on the outside of the window... I was jumping into the bed before my brain could even register that it wasn't my breath causing the moisture.

I heard a light tapping on the window. I must have been seeing something else. Why would a werewolf tap on a window and not just burst through it to eat me? I got up again and crept to the window. I don't know what I was thinking there, if it was at the window, it could see me. No amount of slow movement could stop that. I noticed the sky was a little redder than I had noticed before. Some rhyme about that being good luck for sailors popped into my mind. I put my face against the window again and couldn't see anything; no breathing, no hair, no raccoon, nothing.

Just when my mind slowed down and I was convinced that I had imagined everything, a huge hand lifted from the windowsill and slowly waved back and forth at me. I am a big fan of the *Twilight Zone*. My favorite episode is the one with the monster on the wing of the airplane. I especially like the remade version in the movie. When I say my eyes looked just like John Lithgow's did in the scene where he sees the gremlin's face, I do not think I was even exaggerating a little bit.

I leaped back into the bed and fully committed to not seeing whatever was out there. It had to be huge to block out the window entirely like that. At least double the size of Were-Ted.

Wood began to lightly crack. The sound of the window slowly sliding up on its tracks became a track on a concept album called "last things Marsha heard before she was ripped to shreds by a werewolf."

I closed my eyes as footsteps made their way toward me. I could hear the heavy breathing. It was panting; it had found an easy meal and the excitement inside of its body was too much to contain. This must be why Jack's mom won't eat garlic bread near him. I could smell its odor, completely unlike the other werewolf. This one smelled older, more in control, a bigger threat. If this had been Were-Ted, I would already be ripped apart. This was an old hunter enjoying the thrill of tormenting its food.

Something bumped against the blanket and breathed in. I could make out its snout pushing against my hiding spot. The head attached to the nose was the size of two horses standing side by side. Not the best analogy, but I want to hear what you can come up with in that scenario.

I felt hot breath; I smelled meat caught between teeth. I closed my eyes and held my breath. I had a bad feeling this wouldn't be a quick and painless end. This thing was hunting.

Light filled the room, and Leslie was screaming at the thing. I threw the blanket off my head and ran for the open doorway. I turned around to see Leslie fighting a thing that was so tall it was bent over in the room. Which is no small thing; the ceiling had to be nine feet up. She was pointing and screaming. She took a few intimidating steps toward the thing, and it turned to leap out the window.

When it was gone, Leslie snatched me by my arm, and we ran downstairs into the living room. Jenny and Red were already there.

"Guys," Jenny said. "We have to go get Jack."

I looked at the second floor and sighed. It wasn't going to be me. I didn't want it to be me. But then I realized it probably should be me... hair on my ankle and all.

I contemplated volunteering to go while thinking about how much werewolf I have to be before other werewolves won't try to kill me? I have always wondered that about zombie movies. I guess I just thought it was directly after the bite. That scene a minute ago proved otherwise. Where do these things draw the line between friend and late-night snack?

"That werewolf," I said. Something hit me. "It was terrified of you, Leslie."

"Yeah," Leslie said. She held out a chain around her neck. It was silver with a green emerald. "It's basically werewolf repellent. Pure silver, and this emerald apparently does something to their brains."

I guess that wasn't the most off-the-wall thing I had heard all day. If werewolves exist, they probably have a weakness.

"I could... oh," I said. I stopped volunteering because I saw Red was already coming back down the stairs with Jack. Jack was rubbing his face with agitation and trying to open a bottle of water.

"Bro," Jack said, "please slow down. I am thirsty."

"Okay," Red said. "You want to go back up with the were-wolf?"

"You don't have to be rude, Mr. Stirba."

Chapter 8

Who's Scarier?

"AND IF YOU TELL anyone about that," Jenny said. "I'll not be happy about it."

Somehow this threat had no outcome but was scarier than anything she could have said. There wasn't any or else, no head chopping off, no punching in the face, no burning me alive inside my home.... Just... she wouldn't be happy.

What was she going to be not happy about? I'll explain; I was just setting the moment up with a cool little attention grabber. After Red got Jack and we all let him boo hoo around for a minute about being woken up to avoid being eaten by an actual werewolf, we decided we should play zombie movie and board up all the entrances and exits. Jack tried to tell us all that the strength of a board with nails was no match for the strength of a werewolf. His reasoning was that a werewolf could break the board in half with no issues.

Red admitted he was probably right, and besides, that necklace would do the trick for the most part, wouldn't it? Leslie said it absolutely would, but we should really make sure that the wolf hadn't gotten in anywhere else. A cabin that was as big as a mansion, we would have to make sure there wasn't a pesky werewolf hiding in a spare room or something.

I didn't want to agree, but it was sound logic. If I have watched one movie where people splitting up is a terrible decision, I have watched five thousand of them. It's always the same, someone thinks a bump needs looking into, someone heard a footstep in the attic, someone just can't sleep without checking the lock on the creepy shed that used to be a secret laboratory. Guess what? The monster escaped the lab and was never found... but sure, let's go check it out in the dark. But who am I to argue with conventions in these things. Red used to be a police officer; I would assume he knew what he was doing.

Jenny was wearing a tie-dyed tank top that had Hedorah the smog monster printed on it. I love Hedorah, I think he's painfully underrated, and he is primed for a renaissance to be honest. Off subject, but I will never miss a chance to talk about Hedorah. That unwillingness to pass over a single topic of conversation is what started the events that led up to me wondering how Jenny was somehow more terrifying than her mom.

"Hedorah," I said, "totally my favorite... next to Gigan."

"Me too!" Jenny said. "Although, I think I like Anguirus more than Gigan."

"Hold on," Jack said. He lifted his hands to show us his palms were empty. I guess he wanted to make sure we knew he wasn't holding any weapons for what he was going to say. "You both, as in two human beings in the same room, like Hedorah better than King Ghidorah?"

"Oh yeah," Jenny said. "Monster made from modern pollution and toxic waste is way more relevant than... what? A three headed dragon?"

"Isn't that just a hydra?" I asked.

"Yeah, it is."

"Basic, basic, basic. Of course, the boy likes the hydra the most."

"Something about dragons and masculinity."

"Hey, Red, sweetie," Leslie said. "Tell the girls what your favorite movie is."

"No," Red said.

"Come on," Jenny said. "I know it. But I want to hear him say it."

"I won't say it. Not right now."

"What is it, Mr. Stirba?" Jack asked.

"It's *Dragon Slayer*, okay?"

I laughed so hard my eyes hurt. I needed that. Dragons and masculinity seemingly go together like cookies and milk. How have I never noticed that before? It makes sense on some vague level. Boys grow up reading stories about King Arthur and learn to believe they have to slay some massive beast to win riches and love. To most boys growing up, success is equal to killing a giant fire-breathing lizard.

What does that say about how much Jenny and I love Godzilla, a giant fire-breathing lizard?

Jenny brushed past me to check a door behind me; the room was empty except for a couple of boxes. She closed it and came back by me. When she passed me this time, I noticed something odd. This was the first person I had ever seen growing a long strand of dark brown hair from their shoulder blade. I gasped, Jenny was having some stomach issues too, it made sense. Not that the hair wasn't a look; because it was. It matched the hair on her head and fell across her back in these really nice curls. Lycanthropy comes with its own natural styling and all that; I mean, have you ever seen a werewolf with a cowlick?

"Jenny," I said. "Did that raccoon going through the garbage wake you up?"

"No," Jenny said. "I didn't hear it... where was it?"

"Are you sure?"

She squinted her eyes at me. Her exposed shoulder and what I may have seen hit her brain with the force of a semi hitting a mailbox. Her eyes went John Lithgow in the *Twilight Zone* movie this time. She backed up against a closed door and laughed at me.

"Marsha!" She said; she was totally overdoing the acting. "Come check this room with me and stop worrying about raccoons in the trash! They don't eat pizza!"

"How did you know there was pizza?" I asked.

I felt Jack, Leslie, and Red looking back and forth to both of us in an awkward, tense, and inquisitive way. They must have assumed that we were both crazy already for the Hedorah love; but now they knew we were both better suited for a movie about an asylum in the sixties instead of a werewolf movie.

I shrugged at Jack and tried to laugh. I wanted to present as, "girl who thinks other girl is silly, but what can I do?" But I think I came across as more, "yeah, I'm totally insane too and want to go into a completely empty room to discuss what a raccoon found in the garbage."

When I got into the room, which was totally empty, no joke, no boxes or anything, Jenny slammed the door. She turned to face me and had a newly lit flame in her eyes. This was both parts the Stirba family women's natural intimidation, and her new werewolf thing. She wasn't as good at the first part as her mom, but she would grow into it and be a fierce competitor. Kind of like passing down a wedding dress, but this was passing down the ability to scare anyone, and anything, with a single look. Way better than a wedding dress if I'm being truthful.

"How did you know about the raccoon?" She asked. "And the pizza?"

I bent over and pulled the hair from my ankle so that it was stretched at full length. It didn't curl like her shoulder hair; that bummed me out. I guess it just goes to show how Jen is made to walk out of a house fire looking like she just got styled by a Hollywood makeup artist; where as I'm doomed to walk the

Earth having to spend a few hours every day making myself look like I wasn't in a house fire after going to a spa.

She rolled her eyes and grabbed the sides of her head.

"Ugh," she groaned. "Marty."

"Marty," I said. "Same for you?"

"Yep. I went to a six o'clock showing of some movie he wanted to see. The jerk didn't tell me it was three hours long and had little to no dialogue. I woke up being carried home in the mouth of a werewolf."

"He didn't eat you?"

"Marty would never eat me. Something about my scent, I think. That's why he's terrified of Mom too. He's not quite as afraid of Dad, but he still listens."

"I think Godzilla would be terrified of your mom... Who can blame Marty? What do we do?"

"I'll tell you what I'm going to do. I'm going to say nothing. We have the book the guy wrote—"

"The Were-Ted."

"Excuse me?"

"That's what I'm calling him because it's obvious there are three. Marty, Were-Ted, and this new one. Stomach and head been killing you?"

"Yeah."

"Extra strong senses?"

"How do you think I smelled the pizza?"

I frowned and put my hands on my hips. It was time for me to try and scare a Stirba woman. I couldn't do it without the traditional angry white girl stance of hands-on-hips. I placed those suckers on my hips and leaned into it. Where's the manager because my cheeseburger has pickles and I specifically asked for NO pickles.

"We can't just leave them in the dark on this," I said. "What if we both Kirk out and go all werewolf on them?"

Jenny didn't need to match my stance to be scarier. She just stared me straight in the eyes.

"If you go all Lon Chaney out there," she said. "You better not hurt my family. I assume I'll be the same as Marty when and if I change. I'm probably going to be a werewolf and if you tell anyone about that, I'll not be happy about it."

With that, she stormed off and through the door. She made an instant change from the scariest entity on Earth to a normal happy teenage girl instantly. She would be good at the whole shape shifting werewolf thing for sure.

"It's all good in there!" She said a little too enthusiastically. "No secret hiding places. No werewolves. Nope, not a single werewolf. Definitely not two werewolves that haven't fully changed yet."

I walked out and read the room. Jack and Red were standing beside each other confused.

"To think," Red said. "We're the weird ones because we like dragons."

Jenny shot Jack a look for laughing.

I could feel Leslie shooting Red a look for saying it.

Jenny had Jack scared, but she was a few feet from him. Red being scared was slightly more impressive because Leslie was behind him. He could just feel the rays of annoyance.

"Everything alright?" Leslie said.

"Uh, yeah, Mom," Jenny said. She removed her eyes from Jack, and I swear I could smell his spirit burning up from her stare. "Marsha and me... well... we just needed to talk about something we saw earlier. We didn't know if it would be helpful or not, so we wanted to keep it to ourselves until we decided."

"And the verdict is?"

"We think there are three werewolves here. Marty, Were-Ted—"

"What?" Jack said.

"Were what?" Red asked.

"Pardon me," I said. "Heaven forbid a girl make up a nickname for a werewolf I guess."

"Three?" Leslie asked shaking her head. She was trying to shake my bad nickname from her hair like it was a loose leaf on a fall day and she had just left the hairdressers.

"Yeah," I said. "The one upstairs was more of a red."

"Hey," Red said. "I'm not anything like a werewolf..."

The joke fell pretty flat. Finding out you're trapped at a camp with three werewolves may not be the ideal time to tell a dad joke. Unfortunately, if there is one thing I've learned, dads are going to make dad jokes. It's an impulse they cannot resist. They are unable to can. In the same way that if boys have nothing else, they have the audacity… if dads have nothing else, they have white New Balance sneakers with grass stains and dad jokes.

I think I would still rather be a werewolf than be caught out in public in grass-stained shoes. Just change them after you mow or buy a special pair. It isn't rocket science.

"We also noticed something else," Jenny said. "We can probably get to the van fairly easily. It's a straight shot from here to the bottom of the hill. That new one was scared of your necklace something awful. When we were talking about the raccoon, it was because we both noticed it spilled a box filled with silverware out onto the ground. Get it? Silverware. SILVERware?"

"I think we got it, sweetie," Red said.

"Why else would someone throw out forks and spoons unless they were a werewolf and it burnt their little handy wandy when they wanted to eat their cereal?"

"You're right," Leslie said. "It had to be real silver."

"Guys," Jack said. "Is silverware even really silver?"

"In some cases," Red said. "I don't know if a summer camp is the place it would be though. But it's a good observation, and a good takeaway. Are you sure you don't want to go into the force, Jen?"

"Positive," Jenny said. "I would never stop anyone for speeding."

"Alright," Leslie said. "Let's go scoop up those spoons. It'll be really knife to stick a fork in this place."

We all laughed at these jokes. Mom jokes must be better than dad jokes. Also, Leslie is really scary, I don't know if I've mentioned that.

Jenny saved us more than once that night with some quick thinking. But I have to give it to her, that little bit to get around our conversation was a stroke of genius equivalent to the kid in *Troll 2* realizing Nilbog is Goblin spelled backwards.

Hopefully we didn't get the silverware and realize silver was just "you're an idiot who is going to be eaten by a werewolf" spelled backwards.

Chapter 9

Get the Good Silverware

WE LOOKED THROUGH A window in the back room of the cabin. The silverware was on the ground, totally untouched. The mental confusion I went through was unreal. One second, I was thinking that if I were a werewolf I would definitely move silverware that I knew could kill me... but also... I was fully away that the thought was fundamentally silly. Not really silly, just stupid. If they wanted to move the silverware because touching it could kill them... they couldn't logically move the silverware, could they? And I'm almost one hundred percent sure werewolves don't know how to use any sort of tools or problem solve. They aren't using a shovel or rake is the point I'm making. If they can't solve it with claws, teeth, and an angry demeanor... the mystery has to be beyond them.

Still, I felt that just leaving them there like that had to be a trap of some kind. I think the main issue I was having is that I was trying to apply logic to an illogical situation. Werewolves probably are not aware enough of silver as an object to be able to figure out a creative way to move it. It probably works more like bug spray or poison for them. They must sense the disturbance in the air. Something to do with atoms, matter, and all of that stuff I skipped last year.

To be fair, I didn't really skip it. I just don't know if telling students pages in a book to read with questions to answer at the back is really conducive to learning. The issue I had with that style of teacher is I found myself memorizing the answers instead of understanding why they're the answers. I can tell you all day that plants use photosynthesis, but that is not the same as knowing what photosynthesis is or how and why plants use it. See what I mean?

Maybe the third mystery werewolf was out there having the same struggle. It knew something in the trash was repelling it, but it didn't know why or how. For all it knew, the pepperoni was really spicy, and this particular werewolf suffered from severe heartburn. My dad has that, and you should hear him groaning after a stuffed crust pepperoni lover's pizza. It's rough.

All of this information piled onto a page for no reason other than to point out what should have been obvious: I don't really need to know the "why" of how silver hurts werewolves, I just need to keep in mind that it does. Which is also why I was trying to make an excuse as to why I wasn't going to be the one going outside for the silverware. I guess Jenny wasn't either. It would hurt us, and our secret would be out. That probably explains how the werewolf disposed of it... duh... They're human too. Luckily for us, Jack volunteered to do it.

"No," Red said. "Why on Earth would I let any of you kids go out there? I'm a former police officer. I have been trained in this kind of thing; crisis scenarios. Why would I send teenagers out into a dark area with a werewolf while I stayed inside? Sheesh... the nineties... all of this Nickelodeon has you all thinking that life is one great big TV show and you're the main characters. I will go, and Leslie will watch the door with her necklace."

I can admit it... I was overthinking our roles in the is scenario. This was real life, not a book called "Slime Monster from Ontario" or something. Those sorts of books always make it seem like the teens are saving the day. I think to make it more relatable to the teenaged reader. But wouldn't it be more relatable to just say the truth? That most of the time adults think they're smarter than us? Funny how that works. I've spent my whole life outsmarting them in school, but they definitely know more about werewolves than I do. I think even if I caved and told them the truth that Red would still say he understood the situation better.

Fine by me, I thought, *knock yourself out.*

"Can we at least watch the windows?" Jack asked.

"No," Red said. "That's even too dangerous. I want you three to go into the main room and hide."

"I don't know," Leslie said. "Maybe they could all look out different windows and yell if they see something. Could be helpful."

Red bounced his head around to let the hydrating thought soak into his thirsty brain. He finally nodded and agreed. Jack was stationed in a spare room beside the back door, Jenny was in the main room watching out the front window, and I was blessed with the window over the sink in the kitchen. If you have ever watched *The Legend of Boggy Creek*, you can understand why that was a curse to me. All I could picture was a werewolf's hand reaching up over the windowsill and smashing through. I was surely a goner.

I stood at my spot and scanned the tree line slowly. I didn't see anything remotely like a giant bipedal wolf, so I gave a thumbs up to Leslie. She opened the door and Red stepped out. The trash box was probably thirty feet away from the back door. With three werewolves out there somewhere, that was more like thirty miles.

Red stepped outside into the grass. He looked around and pushed his back against the outside wall. As he moved toward the box, he would pause every now and again to scan with his eyes and ears for anything out of place. The process was agonizing.

He made it to the silverware and started scooping it up at exactly the same time that I saw a blur move in the woods. It was tall, gangly, and fast. It moved toward Red in a side-to-side motion covering more ground than it needed to. I guess that was a hunting strategy; keep your prey guessing about your location and the distance between you both.

I tapped on the window. When Red looked my way, I pointed at the woods. He immediately saw the moving blur. He decided the whole wall shimmy thing wasn't necessary anymore and started running. Personally, I thought the shimmy was silly in the first place. I think he was trying to impress everyone with police tactics. He was also guilty of the same crime as myself: trying to apply logic to an illogical situation. I can't ever fault him though; when we get out into these insane situations, of course we use things that comfort us. That wall shimmy was a comfort move more than one that made any sense strategically.

He had two handfuls of silverware all the way up until he tripped over something and had no handfuls of silverware. Knives, forks, and spoons all flew from his hands and landed in front of him. The sound of silver against silver felt like the opening band at a concert where the headliner was called Tooth Against Bone. Red had to be about to become kibble for the worst dog on Earth.

Jenny ran past Leslie and threw something toward the rushing blur. The blur froze and stared at her. I could see this was the one from my room; it was at least three foot taller than the others and looked twice as mean. It had hair that was more of a reddish brown than a dark brown. It bent lower and lower to the ground while it stared at Red.

Red kept gathering up the loose silverware in his hands and stumbling forward. He managed to get his feet under him and yell at Jenny to get in the house. As soon as he gained some level progress, the wolf was behind him. It hit him in the lower back with the top of its head and sent him falling forward a few feet. He bounced off the wall and rolled onto his back.

I turned on the water in the sink to full blast hot. I grabbed the spray nozzle attached to the side of the sink and shot it into the sink. I could tell it was hot; someone bought the good hot water heater. I opened the window and leaned outside.

"Hey!" I yelled. "Summer heat got you down?"

I thought that was a really cool thing to say right before I opened the stream of hot water. The wolf turned to me just in time to see steaming hot water heading for its face. It didn't have time to move and ended up clawing at its own face to try and alleviate the sensation of burning that was all of a sudden a huge problem.

It dove toward me blindly and fell below the window. I opened the stream again and blasted it across the back.

"Hey, ugly!" Red yelled. I looked because I have kind of low self-esteem. The wolf looked because it was a vain creature and did not like being accused of being unpleasant on the eyes. It dove at Red faster than anyone could follow. It hovered over him as he lay on his back looking up. I wonder now if he was thinking that he should have run away first before yelling? I at least had the boiling hot water gun thing thanks to modern dishwashing technology; all Red had was a bad plan and scattered silverware.

I was preparing to yell again when I saw Leslie step out of the doorway and shove the necklace into the wolf's face. It jumped backwards a few feet and almost tripped over its own tangled feet. Red leaped to his feet and threw a fork at the thing. The prongs got lodged into the beast's matted hair and dangled from its left cheek. The wolf clawed at it and began to pull its own hair away from its face in clumps. I could smell smoke and burning hair, steam raised from the spot the fork was stuck. The werewolf turned and ran back into the woods making a loud whimpering sound.

Red fell into the door and dropped the silverware all over the floor.

"That boot tripped me!" he said. "One of Marsha's pink ones. It wasn't there when I went out. One of them must be upstairs now."

Just as he said it, we all looked up at the ceiling. It must have been hiding really well up there because none of us heard it or saw it move outside. I would miss my new boots, but no amount of confidence was worth going outside for them.

"Okay," Leslie whispered. "Now what?"

"The car keys are upstairs," Jenny said. "Dad asked me to hang them up by his hat."

"Red," Leslie said putting her hand on her head. "You didn't bring that awful hat did you?"

"It isn't awful," Red said. "It's lucky. Do you know how many fish I've caught wearing it?"

"Does it have a dragon on it?" Jack asked.

"Worse," Jenny said. "It has a skeleton on a motorcycle, and it says 'moto-psycho.'"

"Yeah, that's pretty bad, Mr. Stirba."

"I found it on the sidewalk," Red explained. "And then I won free breakfast at the diner. Then I caught the biggest bass you'll ever see—"

"A bit of an exaggeration," Leslie said.

"Either way," Red said as he pointed toward the sky. "We gotta go up there. We know another one is there. We need those keys. They're by my lucky hat. I think you all better hope it was really blessed by some ancient luck genie."

I don't think a "luck genie" or whatever it is would bless a hat and leave it on a random sidewalk, and I also thought we were all pretty "moto-psycho" for going upstairs... but at that point... a lucky hat that was mega-ultra-embarrassing was just about our last hope.

Chapter 10

Unluckiest Hat of All Time

Do you want to hear about another horror movie decision faux pas we committed? Sure, you do. In every movie, the killer or monster chases the victim. The victim always falls; Red did that. The victim always runs upstairs if they live in a house with a second floor. One small complaint I have about that is horror movies have given me a complex about houses. I think everyone lives in a house with two floors. Thanks to movies, seeing a single-story home feels like seeing something totally unfinished to me. My brain asks when the people are going to put the second floor on. Weird, right?

We did the whole going upstairs thing. Why not? We had already split up, fallen, hidden in the killer's home, had a couple plot twists, and found some book with history about the killer. At this point, not going upstairs would be just plain offensive to all the parties involved in this nightmare.

I'm not sure why we all went though. That was a choice if ever there were a choice. We weren't thinking clearly at all. But I guess knowing you're being stalked by three werewolves can have that effect on a person. If a person is fine with the scenario, I'm thinking either this isn't their first rodeo, or they may be a werewolf. Late-stage werewolf, I should say. I was a werewolf and so was Jenny, I think, but we were not okay with any of this.

We all walked slowly up the stairs. Jack was breathing so loudly that I think he had set up some sort of microphone system. He was behind me, at the very back of the line, I turned to him and put my finger to my lips telling him to hush. He lifted his arms in confusion.

"You're breathing too loud," I whispered.

"Oh, sorry," he said. "I guess I'll just stop breathing."

"If you don't be quiet," Jenny said. "a werewolf is going to make sure we all stop breathing."

Good point, Jenny, good point.

The upstairs was much quieter than I expected it would be with a werewolf traipsing around. One would expect some loud huffing, worse than Jack; some heavy footfalls, maybe even some scratching and clawing? We had none of it. It was eerie. I pictured a giant werewolf hiding behind a dresser waiting for us to appear so it could scare us. I couldn't help but laugh at the thought. Imagine, his long and lanky body all hunkered down waiting on us. He was probably getting impatient and having an internal debate about what to do.

I giggled a little loud and covered it with a fake cough. The kind of thing you do when you and a friend can't stop laughing in class. Jenny turned to me and a smile cracked across her face. *Oh no,* I thought, *the giggles must be contagious.* Jenny did the giggle cough thing too.

"Oh, but I'm the loud one," Jack whispered.

We were coming toward Leslie and Red's room, and I couldn't stop thinking about it. What if he was in there hiding behind the bed and all we could see would be his eyes peeking over? That part almost creeped me out, but then I pictured his feet being under the bed and that got me for some reason.

I tried to hold it back, but the laughter came out as a whistle. That was all Jenny needed too; she started laughing uncontrollably. I didn't even try to stop then. Jenny and I were both in tears laughing while the others stared at us with anger and confusion.

"I guess we don't need to be quiet anymore," Leslie said. "Hey! Is there a werewolf up here?"

Nothing responded.

The wolf must have fled the scene.

"I'm sorry," I said. "All I can picture is a giant werewolf hiding and waiting on us so it can jump out and scare us."

"Whoa," Jenny said. "I don't know why or how, but I just knew that's what you were thinking, and I couldn't unsee it."

"Picture this: he is still hiding and heard us making fun of him—"

"AND THEN HE WALKS OUT HERE LIKE 'HELLO, HI, HERE I AM!'"

We both exploded with laughter. Even Leslie started to laugh at that one. When Leslie started, Jack and Red jumped in. I guess they were waiting for her permission. It felt good; I think all of us needed the situation to take a break for a minute.

Red went into the room; we heard the jangle of keys, and he came back wearing his hat. Jenny and Leslie were right; it was an embarrassing hat. To make matters worse, it was bright red. The only people I ever see wearing hats are weird kids at schools and people who want attention. We get it, you have a bright color on your head. The only people who wear red hats are annoying. They probably also order fajitas.

"Whoa," Jack said. "Rad hat, Mr. Stirba!"

Red tipped the bill toward Jack like he was wearing a cowboy hat.

"It's really embarrassing because of your name," Jenny said. "Red wearing a red hat."

"Hey," Red said. "Would you say that to someone wearing an orange hat? No, because you probably won't ever meet someone named orange."

Jack laughed because of course he did.

"Let's all go get dressed a little better," Leslie said. "Then we can try and make it to the car."

I went in my room and did just that.

That was when I knew who the third werewolf was.

"Hey, guys," I said as I came out of my room. "I think I know who the new werewolf might be."

I pointed down to my pink cowboy boots that were definitely not thrown out of a window.

"Yeah," Jenny said, "they're nice. We know."

"No," Jack said, "she wears them because... oh."

"Yeah," I said.

"What?" Jenny said. "What? What? What? Is anyone going to explain?"

"It's Anne Ambrose."

"The TV reporter woman?" Red asked.

"One and the same."

"Okay," Leslie said. "Please explain this one. What is she doing? Is she out here making a special report? An undercover news report about werewolves?"

"Ugh," I sighed. "She went missing here, remember? It says it in Were-Ted's diary."

"It's a journal," Jack said. "Boys keep journals. Only girls write in diaries."

"Jack," I said. "You have a diary. You literally write 'dear diary' at the start of every entry."

"Dear journal doesn't sound as good. Alliteration and all of that, you know?"

"Sure, Jack," Jenny said. "Weird moment of male enforced gender norms aside; why would she come back to the place she was turned into a werewolf?"

"I don't know," I said. "I'm not a werewolf expert."

"Clearly."

I locked eyes with Jenny. She was annoyed about something and taking it out on me. I brushed off the comment and moved on with my train of thought. Knowing who the third werewolf was did us no good. Marty would listen to Leslie, but that wouldn't help us with the other two at all. Knowing we were being stalked as a potential meal by my hero who was now a werewolf wasn't going to make us not a potential meal. it's like when people tell Jack professional wrestling is fake; he always says, "a guy knowing he's going to fall off a ladder doesn't magically make it not falling off a ladder."

"Do you think that knowing who she is can help us in any way?" Red asked. "I don't mean that in a condescending way. Sometimes knowing who the criminal is has helped me. Then we could figure out their traits and the way they behaved. Is there anything that we know about Anne Ambrose that we can use?"

"No," I said shaking my head. "She's basically perfection in human form."

Hero worship is weird. I think Anne Ambrose could do anything and I would make an excuse for her. Here she is, being a werewolf that wants to eat all of us, and I'm still calling her perfect. Just short of being mean to kittens, I don't know what's worse than actively trying to eat someone. In my head, it isn't her fault; she's a werewolf... that's what werewolves do... nature and the circle of life, right?

"Hold on," Jenny said. "She is currently actually—"

"I know," I interrupted. "I just can't think of any weakness she would have. She's a news reporter, not Superman."

"He was a news reporter," Jack said.

"Okay?"

"Just saying. Maybe she is Superman."

"Yeah, okay," Leslie said. She shook her head when she said it to recalibrate her brain after what Jack said. "When Anne Ambrose isn't doing the five o'clock news, she's eating people. Got it. We have no information that can help us. Back to the spoon plan."

"Maybe we should check in the diary?" Jenny said.

"Journal," Jack added.

"It's a diary, Jack. When did you all of a sudden decide to be so macho? Get over yourself. Let's go skim read that thing and see if anything helpful is in it. A guy looks at one bad hat and all of a sudden, he's a stereotype."

I mentally thanked Jenny for putting Jack in his place. When we made our way downstairs, I was behind Jenny. I could see a spot on her back that was starting to bubble up like a blister. Something moved underneath the skin.

"Jenny," I said when we reached the first floor. "Will you go to the bathroom with me? I'm scared."

"Who wouldn't be?" Jenny said. "Yeah, let's go."

When we were inside, I spun her around by her arms and touched the blister.

"Don't!" she said. "I had one on my stomach."

She lifted her shirt a little and I saw a small patch of hair covering a weird-looking grey patch of skin. When I say "weird-looking" it's because I don't know how else to describe it. It looked like elephant skin but covered in grease. It was shiny, bumpy, and thick. The hair that came from it was thick and brown.

"You have one," Jenny said as she pointed to my forearm.

There was a blister. It wasn't as big as the one on Jenny's back, but it was there. Something moved underneath it, and I reflexively scratched at it. I broke the skin and peeled it away. It was dry underneath except for the odd moisture on my skin. It was exactly like the spot on Jenny's stomach.

"Were-Ted's diary says the whole thing is the strongest at midnight," Jenny said. "It's ten o'clock. I bet we'll be fully changed at midnight."

I looked at my arm and shivered.

"See, you're not the only one making discoveries," Jenny winked at me and playfully punched my shoulder when she said it. "Let's go see what's in this diary that is a diary and not a journal."

Chapter 11

The DIARY of Were-Ted

I'LL SPARE YOU A weird build up to the info. A good reporter presents the information as it is, so here you go...

Day Zero:

I'm writing this before I get into all the changes I'm going through.

I've loved fishing since I was a kid. I don't care if I catch any-thing, I just want the peace and quiet. That peace is hard to find when you live in a downtown Columbus apartment overlooking the busiest street in the city. There are some major bonuses; I can go downstairs and have the best Chinese takeout the city has to offer, I'm twelve feet away from a bookstore, and I never have to worry about being alone with all the nightlife. It's great, and I love it... until I need some time to kick back and reflect.

A close friend of mine told me about this abandoned summer camp not far from the city. She said it had a lake, cabins, and working electricity for some reason. Apparently, the owner doesn't even realize he's still paying the bills. Sounded like a perfect get away for me.

I packed up my fishing gear, a sleeping bag, and a portable DVD player; there was no way I was going to stay at an abandoned camp without watching some cheesy slasher movies from the eighties.

I stopped at a gas station for some snacks and easy to make meals. Weird place; owner was this man who hated the camp and sold mostly stuff that was out of date. His cat was mean too; it didn't do anything but lay there, but I could tell it was a biter. How was he staying in business? He did give me his card so I could call him if I needed any deliveries. That seemed counterproductive considering he didn't want me to go; but okay, Walter Quist, if you're delivering pizza, I'll take your card.

Someone or something was watching me. I knew that as soon as I got out of my car. It's that feeling like you're in a video game and the enemy has targeted you. There's just this invisible line connecting you to the eyes of whatever is watching. I felt it the whole time I set up my camp, the whole time I fished, and the whole time I cooked my fish over a fire.

I kind of assumed it was a stray dog; maybe one someone dropped off. That's my biggest enemy; the person who leaves a dog somewhere because they don't want it. I loathe those people so much that I convinced myself that was what was watching me. Some beautiful, loving, goofy dog that got stuck with humans that didn't have hearts.

When I was done eating, I cooked a couple of the hot dogs I found at the station; surprisingly not out of date and turned into moldy, sickness-carrying tubes of processed meat. I ripped them apart and put them on the plate I used for my dinner. When I lay down to sleep, I set them outside on the cabin's porch so that the abandoned pup could eat. Voila! I'd have a new friend. I don't know if my apartment allows pets, but I'll worry about that later was my mindset. Sounds like a problem for future Ted.

I woke up and the cabin was pitch black. I could hear something moving around on the porch. It was scratching at the wooden door with its nails. Had to be a dog, maybe it slept in here and I had accidentally locked it out of its own home.

I stood up, grabbed my flashlight, and opened the door. I was pointing the light toward the ground, right at the level I thought a dog would stand. The only thing I saw was two of the biggest feet I've ever seen covered in red fur. I slowly moved the light upward, fully expecting to see Bigfoot selling cookies or something. The thing kept going... it was at least seven feet tall, probably more.

The light hit the creature's face, and I gasped. This was a werewolf. It had pointy ears, a long snout filled with teeth, and one big appetite for little me. I tried to slam the door, but it lunged forward and clamped its teeth around my upper right arm. It turned to run, and I assumed I was done for. It dragged me off the porch and through the grass. I could feel my back getting scraped up as I was pulled. I clawed at the air around me, searching for anything. I found some sort of metal rod and swung it hard at the thing. I hit it between the ears, and it let me go. I stood up and ran as fast as I possibly could back to the cabin.

I locked myself in and hid. Maybe it would forget about me after a bit. No such luck, it prowled around outside all night. It was only a few hours before the sun came up, but those few hours were filled with a huffing beast trying to get into my cabin.

I packed my stuff that morning and fled as fast as I could. I didn't stop to tell anyone what happened, not even Walter Quist, esteemed salesman of expired goods. Who would believe I was attacked by a werewolf?

I went back to my apartment and noticed strange things happening. I had blisters filled with hair, my senses were turned up to a million (I could smell General Tso's chicken from my apartment like I was in the kitchen), I could feel my body shifting and changing.

At midnight, my whole body cramped. I closed my eyes and shuddered from the pain. When I opened them, I was in the cabin it all started in again.

Ted talks about his first few days at the camp after this. Explaining how he became more and more aware of his change and that he was the wolf. He explains hunting as the beast and resting as the man. I don't feel like that's extremely important to us right now; we've all seen a hundred werewolf movies, you get it. And if you haven't, go to your local video store. I'm positive they have a VHS or DVD copy of one of the greats. One bit of advice though, you want the one where the werewolf visits London and not Paris. Anyway, He ate and acted like a wolf. That's about it. But on day ten, something interesting happens...

Day Ten:

I woke up to a note nailed to the front door of the cabin today. It was from the reporter that went missing that I talked about earlier. It read:

"Hi, I'm Anne Ambrose. TV news reporter extraordinaire by day, werewolf by night. That would make a good show, wouldn't it? Or at least a series of comics. 'Anne Ambrose: Werewolf reporter. She's sniffing out the criminals and taking a bite out of crime!' I bet someone would buy it.

So, yeah, I'm sorry.

That was me at your door that night.

I've been coming here to keep myself and everyone at home safe when I change. I've sort of figured out a way to control what I do when I'm the wolf. I only change once a week now; two times if it's been a stressful week.

I can help you.

I'm going into the city to get some books for you. I didn't expect you to be here; leaving this note so you'll stay.

Stay, doggy, stay."

The joke was irritating. Why was this woman having a laugh about us being werewolves? She's literally ruined my life. Stay here? Let her help me? No way. I need to go back to the city and get some actual help. You know the kind? Like from a doctor?

I shuddered at this entry. This had to be written right before he messed up Jenny's world. I wanted to talk about what I had read with the Stirbas, but they were all keyed up about getting to the van. And I'll be honest; I wasn't going to ruin that motivation. With an escape, there comes safety from being eaten. But also, with that escape comes Jenny and Marsha becoming werewolves and eating everyone else unless we tell them. That's going to be an amazing conversation, isn't it? "Oh, hey, Mom, Dad, what's for dinner? Hamburger Helper? Oh, hamburger help me, not again! WAIT NEVERMIND! I'M A WEREWOLF! YOU ARE WHATS FOR DINNER! HAMBURGER HELP *YOU!*"

I wanted to keep reading the journal. I wanted to convince myself and Jenny we needed to have this conversation.

I was out of time at the moment.

It was fork time.

Chapter 12

Go Fork and Conquer

RED RAN THROUGH THE open door and went for it with forks held out like swords. His confidence was inspiring. He was absolutely confident about his forks.

Poor Jack had a spoon.

How did he get so unlucky?

What was he going to do? Scoop at the werewolves' skin? We all had silverware in our pockets, but for added effect we carried one piece like a weapon. Jack was just the unfortunate one that grabbed a spoon.

Leslie had a butter knife, and I promise you that any of us could have been wielding a sword and not been as scary as she was with that butter knife. That's called aura and I wish I could bottle it up in old milk jugs and sell it.

Jenny and Red had forks. I think the three of us went with the most logical choice of weapons. A butter knife is really just a flat stick, and a spoon is… well… just downright not good for fighting werewolves.

When we ran out of the front door, I was fully prepared to run full force into Were-Ted or Anne. We had yet to see Marty, but I knew full well he was somewhere waiting to strike. Maybe he wasn't getting himself mixed up in this mess on account of it being his family? Either way, Jack with a spoon running down a gravel-covered hill had to be easy pickins so I was surprised Marty didn't at the very least snatch him up.

The gravel kept slipping under my feet. I was waiting to fall down, but I luckily was not the first to do that again.

"Crud!" Red yelled out. He was sliding on his butt down the loose gravel. His hands were trying to stop his forward momentum, but the rocks were not cooperating. He got to his feet just as Were-Ted launched from the woods and landed where he was.

I moved my feet faster, the gravel slipping each time my foot set down. I was probably going to be the next one to fall. These cowboy boots weren't the best for this kind of thing; who thought cowboy boots were going to be the best footwear for a summer camp anyway? I didn't even bring a backup pair.

We made it to the first cabin, about halfway down the hill. We got in front of the door just in time for it to explode outward. Marty launched off the porch on all fours and joined Were-Ted in the chase.

"Crap!" Jack yelled as he slid into a fall. He was in the middle of the pack, so he took out Jenny behind him, who then took out Red who was in the back. Leslie stopped to turn around and save her family, which caused her to slip and fall too. She landed with her arm outstretched collecting gravel in her skin as she slid. I tried to slow down, I was beside Jenny when she went down, instead I slid to the ground when I saw Anne waiting for us at the bottom of the hill.

The three wolves moved slowly toward us; knowing they had us cornered, they took their time. Marty snipped at Were-Ted; Anne growled at both of them forcing them to calm down. Jenny grabbed my hand. We made eye contact, and she followed a sigh with a shrug. *Yeah,* I thought, *we tried, I guess.*

"Okay!" Leslie yelled. She started pulling silverware from her pockets and tossing it off to the side of the gravel path. "I'm done. This was all fun and games for a bit, but now my arm is all scraped up and hurts. I didn't sign up to run down a gravel hill at full blast with a bunch of silverware in my pockets. Red, I don't know why you made us do this."

"Sorry," Red said. "I got a little carried away with the role."

The wolves all stopped walking toward us, crouching down on all four limbs and into a weird sitting position. Leslie stood up and started brushing the gravel from her side and under arm.

"What..." Jack started to say. "I'm..."

"I'm confused," I said.

Jenny sighed and stood up. Red patted me on the head as he passed by.

"Sorry, guys," Jenny said with a shrug. She crossed her arms and looked at the ground as far off to the left as she could so that she wasn't facing us. "This is my fault. I asked Mom and Dad if I could bring you guys. I've known I was a werewolf for a few months now. My first change has just been taking longer than expected."

"Stupid crap," Jack said as he stood up. "All of it! The running, the hiding, the falling, the being so scared I can't breathe... the expired food! Why did you bring me!?"

"Because I'm a werewolf too," I said.

"Oh, can it, Marsha. Everyone can see that. Feel the back of your head."

I reached back and ran my hand through my hair. By hair I mean the thick brown hair and thick skin that was covering the back of my head. I felt around my cranium and guided my fingers across the tips of my pointy ears. I wanted to freak out, but instead I just rolled my eyes. Why wouldn't I notice that? What a total cloud jockey.

"I'm guessing your parents are werewolves too?" Jack asked.

"Yeah," Jenny said. "They've been changing for a while. Mom found the way Anne was controlling it. Poor Marty can't. Apparently, it's like hiccups; if I get scared bad enough, or my adrenaline gets going... it'll force me to change. It worked; I'm changing. So is Marsha. The full moon makes it way stronger too. Mom and dad wanted to make sure we could watch her when she changed the first time so that her whole family didn't get changed like mine."

"I don't care about any of that!" Jack shouted. He turned away from us and pretended to yank hair from his head. He bumped into Were-Ted with his left shoulder and kept walking.

"Your breath stinks!" He yelled at Were-Ted. He turned around and faced us. "A basketball team of werewolves with one not-a-werewolf teenager. What could go wrong? Gee, I don't know, maybe you all would eat me? Was that the plan? Am I just a little quesadilla or something to you all? Made with Col-by-JACK cheese? Well, I'm sorry to say it, but I'm pepper-jack now because I'm mad and feeling a little spicy!"

With that astounding metaphor, he stormed off up the hill toward the house.

"We're going to have to buy him a lot of snacks to make up for this," I said. "Well, you guys will... I didn't know either. I appreciate the sentiment of watching out for me... but I'm with Jack... the rest of it wasn't necessary."

I turned to storm up the hill with Jack. I was guessing the temper tantrum we were about to throw would go down as the stuff of legends. It's weird how we both went from being afraid of the werewolves to being annoyed at their dumb little plot. I guess that's just the wavelength Jack and I live on. It was clear they didn't want to hurt us after all of that. Marty was even standing there kicking rocks around because the situation was so awkward; not really the behavior of a vicious man eater. I think me and Jack were both tired, hungry, and feeling like we had just been taken advantage of.

"Hey, cowgirl," I heard a familiar voice. I turned and Anne Ambrose was standing there in the flesh. She was wearing a sundress that was striped with teal and pink. Her red hair was pulled back into a ponytail. On her feet, pink cowboy boots... that part made me smile.

"I'm sorry," she said. "Jenny told me about how you look up to me. That's why I'm here. I sort of like, kind of, accidentally, may have caused this. I bit Ted, he tried to get to town but got in a bit of a skirmish. He didn't make it to the hospital. They've been waiting to tell you about that part. Red was on patrol and saw him struggling to walk. He wasn't far from home, so he took him to—"

"Leslie," I said. "A nurse. He attacked all of them, didn't he?"

"Yeah, and now Red feels really guilty about all of it."

"He should. It's a weird thing that I'm realizing that what actually happens when you try to help people isn't anything good. You just end up surrounded by werewolves! What's next? You're going to tell me you can see the future and the kid who played Toby in that one episode of *Life's Work* grows up to be a spy and then marries a pop icon?"

I crossed my arms and slammed my foot to the ground. I was trying to look really annoyed and scary, but I felt one of my ears up top twitch like a concerned puppy. Leslie started to giggle, and I couldn't stop myself from doing the same thing. It was a little too specific of a reference.

"I get it," I said. "But why lie? Why not just tell me the truth and leave Jack out of it?"

"Jenny wanted you both here," Leslie said as she walked up the hill. "Red asked us to tell a different story about Marty. He thought you wouldn't think we were all werewolves... and..."

"He feels bad," I said. "Doesn't want me to think he's a bad person."

Leslie shrugged and crossed her arms.

It didn't really make as much sense as I wanted it to. But does anything when you really get down to thinking about it? We all do weird things when we feel horrible about the consequences of our own actions. Heck, one time I lied and told my mom that a giant cat with razor sharp claws attacked the couch and that was why there were two perfect slices on the arm. Not the truth... that I watched a Kung-Fu movie and wanted to practice throwing stars. I definitely left out the bit about my throwing stars being her new kitchen knives that I had duct taped together. Red probably felt like he ruined his family's entire life. That weight was probably incredibly hard to carry every day, especially when one of them can't control what's happening to his body. Red didn't do anything wrong though; he was trying to do the right thing. The world isn't made like a set of balancing scales. Sometimes doing good doesn't provide a good outcome. Sometimes doing good gets your whole family turned into blood thirsty giant canine jerks.

I looked at Jenny down the hill sitting beside her dad. He held his face in his hands. Marty sat beside him with his wolf head resting on Red's shoulder. I shifted my vision to Anne; here was my hero making it her responsibility to help me and the Stirbas. After all that, I still felt mad at them all... until I looked at Leslie.

The vulnerability I saw in her face that night in the bathroom. The night Marty bit me, nonetheless. It was there times twenty. She looked crushed. She was a mother trying to do what was best for her family. She didn't know what to do. Who would? Her son changed into a wolf every night and her daughter was a ticking time bomb of werewolf waiting to explode and attack everyone. All she knew was her daughter wanted these two dumb monster-movie-obsessed kids to be her friends; and one of those dumb kids went off and got bitten by a werewolf too. Leslie was just trying to make sure her daughter was safe both physically and emotionally. To her, this weird scheme was a good option.

"We were going to tell you," Leslie said to me. She had tears in her eyes. "We just thought with Jack here, maybe you and Jenny would feel comfortable. We're really trying to make things so we can all safely live together. There are a lot of us like Ted who are hiding. I didn't want you or Jenny to be like that. You see how Marty is with us. I thought maybe with a human connection—"

"To someone we loved, we would control the wolf," I said. Makes an odd sort of sense. In a world where werewolves exist, I guess that was as good a plan as any.

Sure, why not?

"Okay," I said. "What do we need to do?"

Chapter 13

Front Porch Heart to Heart

I'M AS MUCH FOR getting to business without any distractions as the next person. Really, I am; my mom says I can't cook because of the opposite... I get distracted by something going on outside and I forget I've got something frying in oil and the next thing I know a chicken patty is on fire in a pan. Word of advice, when this happens to you and your friend Jack, who you were cooking the chicken patty for, yells "sink" do not, absolutely positively do NOT go to the sink. If you do that, and you turn the water on, it will ignite the oil even more. In this case, you will have a fireball shoot past you toward the ceiling and your parents will not be at all happy to have to replace the ceiling and flooring in the kitchen all because your dumb friend likes crispy chicken and you got distracted by a cat playing with a slice of pizza in your yard. It happens.

Those kinds of distractions are the most embarrassing kinds; especially when your mom is an acclaimed chef! Jack would not stop saying things like, "imagine having a mom who has won cooking awards and you can't even make a chicken sandwich!" I was totally not able to *can* in this case. Cooking wasn't my thing. Distractions shouldn't be anyone's thing, but I guess I can put that on a resume one day.

This was a crucial distraction that had to happen though. Poor Jack had to feel more used than I did. He wasn't even here because he was a werewolf; he just happened to have a crush on a girl who was; and be best friends with another girl who was. Jack needs to stop hanging out with girls, I think. It's bad news for him.

He was sitting on the front steps of the house we had just fled. He had another bottle of Crystal Pepsi sitting beside him un-opened. I always know something is wrong with him when he does this. I mean, I've talked about how good of an investigator I am when it comes to noticing things; but I knew something was wrong by the way he stormed off. It didn't take Sherlock Holmes to figure that one out.

I went around the house and in through the kitchen door. I shook my head at the sight of the silverware that Red had dropped. What a goofball... he made all these plans. Boys and dads, who can figure out why they do the things they do? Red would rather run around with silverware putting on some grand show than just say he made one single mistake that he is actively trying to fix. Being a guy must be annoying. I know it's definite-ly annoying to be around them when they're like that. Like, just say sorry, you know?

I grabbed a plastic cup and made my way to the front door. The cabin felt odd now. I had no choice but to remember what happened in here an hour or so ago and get annoyed with Red all over again. Lucky hat, lucky schmat. I walked out and sat beside Jack. I held the empty cup out in his direction and pointed at the Crystal Pepsi. I guess it was time to see what the hype was all about.

"Don't judge it too harshly," Jack said. "It's expired, remember?"

"Sure," I said. I didn't know what to say or how to start this conversation. I was hoping just being there with him and showing him I was present would help him. I know Jack likes a good rant and rave though, so I was hoping he'd get to have one. It was totally his choice though; I wasn't rushing him or pressuring him by nudging his leg and sighing. That's just how I breathe.

"Hey," Jack said. "At least you found a place to fit in, you know?"

"What?" I said. This wasn't the first sentence I thought would fly out of his mouth like an airplane of jealousy targeted at the runway of my heart.

"You know; you and them... you're all going through this together now."

"Jack," I said as I put my cup down and turned to face him. I knew he wouldn't turn, but hopefully me doing so would show I was serious about what I was saying. "You fit in with us too. They've all been through it except me and Jenny; it's technically you're first time dealing with your friends being werewolves... so that makes the three of us in it together."

Jack rolled his eyes and made a fart noise with his mouth.

He's really mature.

"I don't fit in anywhere," Jack said. "I'm a square peg in a triangle hole."

"I think it's a square peg in a round hole."

"Either way," Jack said as he took a sip of soda for effect. "Doesn't fit."

"You're my best friend. I'm positive Jenny kind of likes you too or she wouldn't have invited you. I think she may even LIKE like you—"

"Oh, please. You're such a cloud jockey sometimes, you know that? Clearly, she LIKE likes you, Marsha. And it's pretty clear you LIKE like her."

I laughed.

I couldn't stop.

What was he talking about? I couldn't stand Jen. She was arrogant, annoying, and way too... bright for me. Also, she's a she. Jack doesn't know anything sometimes. Boys don't know anything about hats, so why would I think Jack knew anything about relationships?

"Are you sure this isn't booze of some sort?" I asked him. I picked up the cup and sniffed it then made a gag face for effect. "That's crazy!"

"No, it isn't. And you know it isn't. It's okay, I don't LIKE like either of you. You're my friends. I just hope if you break up, after you eventually get over yourselves and get together, that it isn't this great big awkward thing for me. I don't want to have to be a part of shared custody with you both."

I just sort of nodded my head. He wasn't exactly wrong. I had noticed myself feeling different about Jenny since we got there. I thought maybe I was just understanding why Jack had a crush on her. I needed to think about that a little deeper, but Jack was probably right about that one.

"Okay," I said. "Let's say I LIKE like Jen… There's no way she LIKE likes me, Jack."

"See… you're asking me if I think she does without just plain out asking. She does, for the record… she told me before we went to see *Godzilla*. That's why I invited her. But then you were meaner to her than you were to that thing—the one that was only Godzilla in name, mind you—was to New York City. Honestly, I don't know why they made it look like that. It didn't even—"

"Jack! Okay. Whatever. Thank you. If you're not upset about me or Jenny. What's the issue? How do you not fit in? The whole world is basically non-werewolves. We're non-werewolves most of the time too. You fit in more than I do just on account of being not a werewolf. Like, come on!"

"Do you know what it's like to be a teenage boy who spends all of his time with two girls?"

"No… no I can't say that I do."

"I get picked on by other guys. They call me Mrs. Jennifer or Mrs. Marsha. Don't flatter yourself, but I like the Mrs. Marsha one better because it rolls off your tongue."

"Alliteration."

"Yeah, we are a litter nation in America. It's a real problem. But please don't change the subject."

"No, alliteration. It's when... you know what? Forget it. I see why you're failing English."

"Other boys think I'm weird. And when they're nice to me... it used to be because they liked you... but now it's because of Jen... when I tell them neither of you are interested, they get mad. They say I'm keeping you both to myself."

"Oh, gross! Jack, I think you're better off! Boys are by far the weirdest."

"And everything I like... movies like *Clueless* or *Batgirl* com ics..."

"There is no such thing as a movie for boys, or a book for girls. I like *Predator*. I like *Predator* a lot. Is *Predator* only for boys because it's bad ass?"

"Yeah... I don't know... I'd rather be a werewolf."

"It is kind of cool to think about, isn't it?"

"No. It stinks. Like figuratively and literally. And those weird hair bumps are gross"

"Okay, so now you're good at the conventions of English. Seriously, I'm not going anywhere. Neither of us have ever fit in. That's why I'm stuck going to the movies with you and I wouldn't have it any other way. I've always got you, and you've always got me. It's just that now you have an entire pack of werewolves to do your bidding."

"Yeah... I guess you're right."

We sat there in silence for a minute. I sipped on the clear soda. It was okay, it tasted a little dusty somehow. I don't know how a liquid can taste dusty, but I think it may have been the expiration date talking.

"Hey, Marsha," Jack said. "Thanks for being my friend."

"You're welcome," I said. "Thank you for not making me drink a whole bottle of this."

He took my cup from me and gulped it down. I guess he didn't want to share with me when I didn't appreciate the true greatness of a clear soda that is usually not clear. I'll stick to 7up for clear soda.

"Want to help us investigate?" I asked.

"Yeah," Jack said. "Go ahead of me. I want to sit here and look thoughtful for a bit. Also, I think I need to cry real quick. I'll bring snacks."

I never thought about how it had to be for Jack being my best friend. I never pictured boys noticing me. I'm really resisting the urge to get a little long winded here about how sometimes teenage boys are worse than werewolves, but I think if you're reading this and you've been around one, you already know that. I'll just get to the next part.

Jack sat there stewing in his chicken noodle soup for the teenage boy who had reached maximum sadness. He had hit peak sad. I went on a little detour before I found Anne and

Jenny. We all had a lot to deal with when we made it out of this camp; but I was glad I had a best friend who knew things about me before I even knew them and offered me soda and conversation.

Chapter 14

Investigation Montage!

I KNOW, I KNOW… every story ever has this thing. It's either the montage just starts, or there is some self-referential mention of a training montage. I don't want to do either; I want to tell you about how I got to do research with my hero, Anne Ambrose, but do so in a fun, shortened way that only highlights the important bits.

I think the montage is perfect here. When I watch a movie about how a down-and-out nobody who was bullied beyond belief learns how to be a superhero, I don't want to see them learning how to breathe properly for twenty hours. Show me the important parts of their training so I get the feel that they really worked for it, give me a crazy upbeat song that makes my blood pump, then let me see the final confrontation.

Let's do this:

Since I haven't even begun to explain what the final confrontation even is in this scenario, we need to establish how I even found that out. I don't think just telling you is my best way of giving you the story... remember the turn to A7 conversation? We have a little bit to go still, and I need you to stick around; therefore, you're getting some of the info I had to process to get to what needed to happen, and what did happen.

So, if you like a montage without tongue-in-cheek self-referential *Scream* franchise stuff... just skip the next bit and begin.

If you want the *Scream* stuff...

Here's a fast-paced musical montage showing you how I figured out what we needed to do!

Put in your favorite cassette and let's go! Not anything gloomy though; It needs to be something you can picture people in bright colors lifting weights to. If you can't picture yourself doing a roundhouse kick to a villain's jaw while it plays, it is NOT the tune.

Here we go!

Anne explained to me that she was bitten when she went missing overnight. I don't think you needed a detective to figure that out, but there you go. She said she got lost and decided to wait until the next morning to find a way back. She was woken up by something dragging her through the woods. She kicked it a few times before it ran off, leaving her with one ruined cowboy boot and a couple of small tooth marks in her right foot. That night she changed, and the next morning she woke up outside of the camp. She said she had a crazy bad headache and a weird aftertaste in her mouth. Probably not from hot dogs cooked over a bonfire for dinner. I wasn't going to tell her that.

She explained how she continued to come to the camp to hide, and it was really just Ted's dumb luck that he did it on a night when she had to change. She had managed to control her changes so that she only went once a week, or sometimes only once a month. She would go to the camp when the feeling started, go feral for the night, then go home like nothing happened. One mystery was solved.

Like any good reporter, Anne asked to look through some of the books Ted gathered. Ted had apparently been building up a small collection of resource materials in his room that would help him understand his affliction so that he could better control it. He and Anne wanted to live normal lives and in order to do so they couldn't be kirking out and transforming into a blood thirsty monster every night. I guess that kind of thing is frowned upon by society and makes it really hard to have any sort of life. Good to know for future reference. Not the kind of thing I should put on a resume or college application.

In his little hideaway, we flipped through pages. I took note of anything that seemed remotely important, and so did Anne. When we compared our notes, we found some main points that we needed to focus on. There were some things that didn't make sense to talk about like werewolves having weirdly specific opinions on cooking shows; switching out soap for a three-in-one body wash, shampoo, and conditioner to keep fur looking its best; and of course, werewolves don't like peanut butter. Something about how everyone tricks their dog into taking medicine by covering it in peanut butter. Werewolves do not like to be anyone's fool. The important stuff though...

The change is like sleep—your body needs to do it. You can stretch it out to long periods of time between, but if your stress level is too high, it's going to happen. You have to recharge. It's got something to do with trying to contain a whole other animal species within your mind, body, and soul or something really meaningful like that.

The moon does play a role—it is harder not to change when the moon is full and at its most powerful. It's strongest at midnight; a new werewolf like Jenny or myself will almost certainly have to change then fully if they have already started. No one knows why, maybe the first werewolf was an alien... who knows? Werewolves from outer space hasn't been done has it? Sort of strange, seems like an easy three hundred bucks to make in the home video and rental store department.

Being a werewolf kinda stinks—yeah, we know. Can't live a normal life anymore.

Sometimes werewolves get stuck in a stress to werewolf cycle—the idea of being a werewolf is stressful! I know that first-hand. We decided this is what is happening to Marty every night. He can't handle the stress from knowing he's going to change, so he changes. Sort of a catch-22 really. My dad used to stomp around our house annoyed about how you need credit to make big purchases, but you have to make big purchases to build credit. What a mess human life is... maybe I'd be better as a full-time werewolf.

Werewolves are not immortal—they age just like normal people. That was a huge relief to me. I didn't want to be stuck in my sophomore year for eternity. I've watched a ton of vampire movies and vampires always come across as nerdy history kids. It isn't because they really love history, oh no, it's because they lived in it. Besides, could you imagine a vampire or werewolf going to high school forever? They would have to find adults to pretend to be their parents all the time. It would be a total headache and make having a simple high school crush absolute misery. What if a vampire and a werewolf both had a crush on the same person? I was not looking to find myself in that situation.

There is no cure—people have looked for one for centuries. They've used everything from silver to dog training manuals; it's just not possible. Your only hope is to find a person who has been a werewolf for a long time and ask for advice. Terrible option considering Anne had been a werewolf the longest, and she was receiving information that was just as new to her as it was to the girl who hadn't even changed yet.

We took a break to eat something; I was starting to get a headache, and Jenny said she had one while we were digging through books. Jenny credited the cure to her headache to a package of Pop-Tarts. Makes sense as long as they aren't unfrosted. Unfrosted Pop-Tarts are by far the most pointless thing to exist.

"If we don't know anyone who's been a werewolf longer than Anne," Jenny said. We sat at a picnic table eating our snacks and flipping through books for ideas. "If that's the case, how are we going to control it?"

"I guess we can do whatever I do?" Anne said. "Just come out here whenever it's about to happen?"

"That seems a bit much," I said. "I'm in high school. I can't come out here every single night. No way is that going to work. My grades will tank."

"Yeah," Jenny said, opening a bag of Cheetos. "And I can't train Ms. Megan to just give me A's."

"Ms. Megan, can't train her."

"What about this," Anne said. She lifted her palm up like she had some huge revelation. Imagine my disappointment when she said, "what if we keep cages in our homes?"

"Yeah, Anne," Jack said as he sat down with his own pile of snacks. "That's going to go over well when anyone visits."

"Hey!" Leslie yelled through the open front door. She carried a book with her and brought it to us in a hurry. "Check this out!"

She set the book down in front of me and Anne and opened it to a bookmarked page.

Sighting five - April 1952 - I was hiding in the bushes above the cabins. It looks like the construction crew has gone home. The only person who stayed behind is the owner of the place. I have not introduced myself yet, but I think I need to. Maybe he has seen some of these same things? He's a young guy, so I'm guessing family money bought this place for him.

I was watching the lake, that was the last place I saw the thing. It did not disappoint. I saw a great amount of splashing, and sure enough, there it was holding a fish in its jaws. It sulked off into the woods, and I lost it.

"What is this?" I asked. I closed the book and looked at the cover. It was inscribed with a title and no name, "New species of wolf - Camp Howling."

"This is going to be immensely helpful," Anne said. She immediately opened the book to the first page.

First sighting - March 1952 - The construction crews have been thinning out by my home. They arrived a few months ago to begin building what I've heard should be Ohio's most popular summer resort. They say the lake is an untapped resource that not many know about. The owner is a man in his twenties with a youthful spunk and ambition. He works with the crew every day.

I have been hearing strange noises since they arrived. My son says he hears a wolf outside of his window; my wife refuses to allow any of us to go outside after dark. She claims to have seen the thing. That is what I will consider the first sighting.

Two weeks ago, she was walking our small pet, a tiny fluffy thing that does not stop barking at every noise. She calls the dog Precious, I call it annoying... but yes, a little endearing. The dog caught a scent it didn't like and began to tug at its leash to go inside. My wife did not want to clean up its mess inside again, so she pleaded with the dog to remain calm. From behind her, she heard movement. She claims to have turned and found herself face to face with a creature standing eight feet tall. She ran inside and locked the doors. It caused quite a stir in our home that night, needless to say.

Sighting two - March 1952 - Our son woke us up screaming. I ran to his room as quickly as any parent would. When I opened the door, I saw a face the size of my chest looking into his bedroom window. I screamed as well.

I am sending them to stay with relatives.

"This sounds like our original, doesn't it?" Anne asked.

"I bet it's someone from the construction crew," I said.

"Entry five says they all left."

"Except the owner..."

"Bingo."

"Hate that game," Jack said. "I always get so close to winning. It's always one or two spaces off though. It's really annoying."

He continued to eat some form of snack cake. I didn't have the audacity to tell him he won a couple times; he just didn't notice. I didn't tell him then because I wanted the free movie rental prize. If he didn't win, I would have had a better chance. I didn't tell him at that moment because I would have to rent him movies if we survived. A girl can only watch *Saturday the 14th* so many times.

Then I remembered how bad it felt to be lied to about this whole werewolf thing.

"Jack," I said. "I owe you like five movie rentals. You won, you didn't notice, I didn't say anything so I could win."

"Five times?" Jack asked with his eyes open in shock.

"You won more than that, but if you want those rentals, you need to take it up with other kids that won. They beat me too."

"I think that's fair enough."

He went back to eating.

I went back to reading.

Third sighting - March 1952 - I saw it outside in the trash. It's a massive thing. I have no doubts it would be dangerous if confronted directly. It reminds me of a wasp... if I let it carry on with its business, it will let me carry on with mine.

I watched it for a long while. It stands at around eight feet, it's covered in brown hair, it's bipedal. It is without doubt some form of wolf. I have never witnessed a canine that walks on two legs.

Fourth sighting - April 1952 - It seems to eat fish when there is no garbage. I purposely left the trash from last night in the bin. It came back, sniffed, and then left. I followed a bit before I decided that keeping my distance may be my best bet. I pulled out my binoculars (yes, I know it was illegal to keep anything from the war. But these are nice and come in handy living here) and followed its path. It went to the lake and began to use its hands to catch fish. It ate them in the same way I would eat a snack; a few bites, and it was gone.

"Notice anything?" Leslie asked.

"It's not vegan?" Jack said.

"Look at the sixth entry, and the seventh."

Sixth sighting - May 1952 - It tried to break into my home today. I spoke with the young man who owns the camp; he admitted to hearing noises but being a bit of a deep sleeper. He says his cat is very aware of whatever is outside and tries to escape nightly; every cat I have met is like this, they believe in their heart and souls they could take on five armies at the same time if the need should arise. He is too excited to open next month and is overwhelmed with what needs to be done. I talked with him for a bit about his time in the war; things neither of us ever wanted to reflect upon again. He spent some time separated from his troop and stayed with a carnival of the Roma people for a month or more. The cat was given to him as a parting gift when he managed to find a way back to the states.

After the break-in attempt, I am going to have a reunion with my family. None of this is worth it.

"There is no entry seven," I said.

"That's my point," Leslie said. "He got smart and left."

Anne snapped her fingers. "Do you notice?"

"That the werewolf broke in after he talked to the camp owner?" I asked.

"Yep."

"Who is the owner?"

"Oh!" Jack said. He basically leaped out of his seat to pull something from his back pocket. "I meant to show you this. Remember how Ted knew the gas station guy's name? Check this out!"

It was a brochure with a familiar face on the cover. Only the face was younger... and not selling expired food. That face was selling time at a newly built campground now.

Walter Quist.

"Weird, right?" Jack asked before moving on entirely in his mind.

"We know who to go to now," Anne said.

"Not quite yet," Jenny said. She pointed over her shoulder to the clock.

Ten 'til midnight.

Crud.

Chapter 15

Ch-Ch-Ch-Ch-Changes Turn and Face the Strange

There's a show about a teenage girl in which she turns into a weird mercury looking melty puddle thing and can go anywhere. I don't remember the name of the show; Jack loves it, I prefer *Clarissa Explains it All*. She turns into a puddle and melts, right? So, the bit that has always confused me was how she manages to come back fully clothed. I could think of like maybe one or two things that would be more embarrassing than popping up in the middle of an army base totally naked.

She was always free of embarrassment and dressed for the occasion. All I could think about when midnight hit was how I hoped that I would be so lucky. I know Anne was in her dress and boots when she changed back; but maybe she's just really good at changing outfits? Want the truth?

Here's my expose on changing into a full-fledged werewolf.

Midnight hit and I felt it. I can't explain it. My grandpa used to say if you stretch your legs out when you cross a state line you could feel the line on the map go across your body. It's silly to say, but that's exactly what I felt. Imagine if the Earth were a cosmic kitchen timer; midnight was a loud buzz. I'm still slightly confused by the time thing; taking into account daylight savings, leap year, blah blah blah, how did it work? I just leave it be and try not to pick it a part too much. Maybe it's like a placebo effect for a werewolf?

The time hitting midnight felt to me the same as when you stand up too fast after eating too much ice cream. My brain felt an electric zap, and I almost fell down. I sat down beside Jenny; we held hands and prepared for it together. It was comforting having someone close that was going through the same changes. I didn't like Jenny much before all of this... But maybe Jack was right and I was starting to LIKE like her. I shook those thoughts from my head; like I told Jack, I really had to make this whole werewolf thing my first priority. I could worry about werewolves LIKE liking each other and two girls liking each other as more than friends after I figured out how to do the whole werewolf thing without killing anyone.

I felt skin changing and taking shape all over my body. My t-shirt started to pull against my body. I assumed it was because I was growing in size, but what I saw told me otherwise.

The rough skin from under the blisters was spreading sort of like an exoskeleton. I watched it spread over the top of my clothes from my skin. My sleeve was still out; I pulled on it and the skin lifted with it; I could see my normal skin underneath the sleeve while the new molded to the surface of the shirt. The skin pushed down the shirt sleeve and connected to my skin like a scab.

My stomach started hurting so I looked at my boots. They too were being encased in the new skin; I was beyond worried they would get stained. My eyes felt heavy and when I blinked, I opened them to a different world. I was seeing through a set of glasses that somehow showed me colors that humans have not even thought of inventing. I won't try to describe it at all; that would be impossible. Everyone had a color around them like a glow. Jack's was comforting, but too bright for my eyes; like staring directly into the sun. Jenny's was the one I felt the best looking at. It was a shade of blue and purple that made me feel safe, comforted, and understood. I could have changed everything in the world to the color that radiated from her and never had a bad day again in my life. Her fur was a dark blonde, but I couldn't focus on anything concrete and real when that glow was surrounding her. We made eye contact, and I could sense she saw the same thing when seeing my glow.

I noticed that everyone around me vibrates a little too. Let me explain; Jack was in shock and standing still in front of us, only he wasn't. His body had a slight shaking effect; I thought he was shivering. Looking back, I think I was seeing every separate atom that makes up the person that is Jack as they moved over his body. I could focus on microscopic organisms that were living inside of his pores and see all of their limbs. Jenny was moving on the same pattern as me, but on opposite beats. We were complementing each other's existence.

My sense of hearing went wild. When Jack sighed, I could hear the air traveling through his nostrils. I could hear the bristle of the tiny hairs all over everyone's bodies. I focused on the pore-creatures again; they were communicating with each other in voices that sounded like radio static. Everything had a rumbling sound.

My smell went insane. I could smell a small spot of expired Crystal Pepsi on Jack's shoe. I hate smells so I shook my head and made that sense calm down.

I tried to stand up and woke up six hours later lying in the woods. Time keeps on slipping, I guess. Jenny's head was laying on my shoulder. She was laying on her back using it as a pillow with her body going the other way. The way I felt like something was stolen from me when she sat up told me everything I needed to know about Jack's theory. I did LIKE like Jenny. Great, now I have to figure all of that out too. You would think that would be easier to explain to someone than explaining you were a werewolf... but I've watched enough TV shows to know that's not the case. It wasn't my mom and dad I was worried about; well, with the werewolf thing I was. They'd be fine with the other thing. It was the rest of the world that I feared would be more against this part of me than the part that turned into a monster made of teeth, claws, and irritation trying to eat them. If I had Jenny, and Jenny had me, and we both had our parents, and oddly enough Jack... We could love all the parts that made us up and be confident they weren't bad. The werewolf part was a little not great, but the other thing was perfect and shouldnt have to be hidden at a camp.

"Wow," I heard Jenny say beside me. Her voice broke me away from my internal philosopher. "That was the craziest thing I've ever been through in my entire life. That's saying something. Did you know I've been on every coaster at King's Island and Cedar Point? That was crazier than any of it."

"I..." I started to say. I felt a little goofy because I didn't know how it was all of a sudden daylight. "I don't remember anything past all my senses going rogue on me."

"Same. I felt like Superman, and then I wake up here staring at that bird. It was like reverse. The bird was super easy to see, smell, hear... I could feel it moving the air from up top of that tree. Then it was like my body was a vacuum. I was just going back in it like I was in *Ghostbusters*. I can't even see the branch it was on now."

Jenny pointed upward; I looked and couldn't even see a trace of where a bird might be. It was all tangled branches and leaves.

"How does Marty do this every night?" I asked. "I don't hurt or anything, I just feel really confused. Out of place almost."

"Yeah," Jenny said as she sat up. "The world feels alien to me now. It's going away a little, that feeling, but I feel like I'm on another planet. It's better having you here with me for all of it."

Her smile after she said that told me we were going to be okay.

"Whoa!" I heard Jack's feet moving at the same time I heard his voice. "That was insane!"

He tried to stop running too fast, causing his feet to slide on the ground and fly out from underneath him.

"You both went totally werewolf!" He yelled. I wanted to stop him, and I couldn't see Jenny was about to, but I wanted to know what happened and Jack was going to tell us.

"It was like watching *Power Rangers*! Your faces just vanished! There was like this weird mask that covered you both and then it started moving around like clay being formed. It was crazy! You both looked like you were putting on costumes or something! Then you both took off like a billion miles an hour through the woods. Mr. and Mrs. Stirba sighed and did the same thing you guys did! I tried to keep up with all of you, but it was impossible. I was also sort of scared you guys would eat me! Imagine waking up after eating me!"

"Yuck," Jenny said. "Talk about indigestion."

"Ha ha, you're so funny, Jenny. You wouldn't be laughing if you knew you ate from that dumpster by the entrance last night! You both had like total fish bone fever or something. YUCK!"

I shook my head and laughed. Jack not being scared made me feel a lot better about the whole ordeal.

"We didn't..." I said.

"Hurt anyone?" Jack asked. "Oh... yeah... there was a bus full of elementary school kids you both turned into an all you can eat buffet... NO! You just ran around acting like insane people while the other four tried to get you to calm down!"

"Okay, Jack," Leslie said, walking up. "Are you two feeling okay?"

"Yeah, Mom..." Jenny said.

"I feel odd," I said. "Are there any side effects."

"You've already experienced them," Anne said as she walked up with Red and Marty.

Marty looked way different now. He looked more like Leslie than Red. He was tall still, good for him, I guess.

"Hey, Marsha," he said to me. "Sorry about... all of this."

"It's okay," I said. "We'll figure it out together."

"See!" Jack said. "The side effects!"

"Jack," I said, "I need some type of context please?"

"Okay, so, you know how you're like super mega ultra shy and you can't even talk to me sometimes? Well, I noticed you've been just talking to all of us like it doesn't bother you. You talked to Anne last night without any pause, and just now with Marty. Oh! Hey, Marty!"

"Hi, Jack," Marty said as he helped me up. "I think some of the werewolf's confidence or something is in our human forms when we change back."

"Is that how I was able to be nice to Dad about the dragon thing?" Jenny asked.

"You were nice?" Red said.

"Oh, yeah, trust me. I could have been way worse."

"Were's Ted?" I asked.

"He's trying to figure out why his trap didn't keep him in," Anne said. "He's beating himself up pretty badly about almost hurting you three. Which is silly, I was there the whole time making sure he wouldn't. If he would have gotten too close, I would have tossed him into the lake."

"Knowing he was going to get beat up by a girl in pink cowboy boots may be upsetting him too," Jenny said. "You know how fragile these boys can be."

"Hey!" Jack said.

"Jack," I said, "remember how you reacted when I beat you at *Mortal Kombat*?"

"Ugh! Not this again! All you did was crouch and uppercut!"

"The ends justify the means."

"Okay, whatever, I get it, I guess. Sorry."

"See, now you're kissing up because you know I can eat you later if you make me mad."

"The ends justify the means, right?"

We went and checked on Ted. He was sitting on the ground staring at his little door. He had brown hair, a pair of gym shorts, and a blue t-shirt on. He sported a full beard that looked like it hadn't been trimmed in months.

"Ted," Anne said. "It's okay. No one got hurt."

"Speak for yourself," he said. "My ego is pretty bruised up. I'm sorry, kids, I'm Ted. I chased you around last night."

"Sorry about the skillet," Jack said.

"No need to apologize, it was well deserved."

"What do you guys think?" Red asked. "Should we go have a little chat? Maybe get some expired Twinkies?"

"Do those expire?" Leslie asked.

"I think everything does, right?"

"Now I've always heard…"

And thankfully we were back to more playful bickering and less being chased by something for dinner.

Chapter 16

Daylight Savings

IF IT'S NEWS TO me, it may be news to you... some werewolves can change in the day. I do not believe I have ever watched a single werewolf movie, read a single werewolf book, or watched a single one of those "real werewolf caught on camera" videos and saw anything at all about a werewolf that can just up and change during full-blown daylight. It was like finding out that sometimes cheese comes from bears or something.

"I didn't know we could do that," Anne said to me on the subject when we were hiding behind an old school bus.

Yeah, Anne, I don't think any of us saw that one coming.

Do one of those record scratch rewind effect things because this is how I found myself in that predicament.

Marty and Ted stayed behind at camp when we went to the station. They had some reason that they explained, it could have made sense, but I think it was mainly because they felt like the odd men out here. I knew Anne, so she was a part of it; although, the Stirba's definitely knew Marty better than I knew Anne. I don't know, maybe it had something to do with the van having six people riding already. The duality of man.

When we pulled up, it was just as empty as before. We walked inside and pretended to browse the expired snacks again. Jack grabbed another Crystal Pepsi. What is his obsession? Sprite and 7up have always been clear... Why is it cool because it's Pepsi? Maybe it's sort of like the whole changing in daylight thing. Maybe somewhere in the world a vampire is enjoying a nice loaf of garlic bread.

"What are we doing?" I asked.

"I'm buying snacks," Jack said.

"Okay, sure. But we're not here for that."

"Who even knows when I'll see this again! It's not like it will have some nostalgic come back tour. Besides, when in Rome... I was letting Anne, or Leslie, or Jenny, heck, even you do the talking. I don't want to."

Anne nodded at me and smirked.

A field tryout, huh?

Well, okay then!

I snatched the Crystal Pepsi from Jack and marched toward the counter.

"Hello!" I said. "I would like to purchase this finest and expired Crystal Pepsi. I would also like you to tell me how you became a werewolf, how you keep it in check, and why you didn't tell any of us this?" I grabbed a Cow Tail and pointed it at Walter like a microphone. You know the Cow Tail, right? Like a dessert Slim Jim. Caramel filled with icing, or sometimes this red apple tasting stuff. I like the apple better.

"What did you say?" Walter asked. His cat made a low growl and leaped behind the counter. The door flew open and closed; the cat decided to take a little stroll.

"You know what I said," I challenged. "Walter Quist."

He began to shake. I thought I had accidentally gone off and made him have a medical emergency. I backed up in a hurry and hid behind Leslie. Somehow, a heart attack or whatever was happening had to be afraid of her too, right? She stepped forward and stared at Walter without blinking. It was terrifying.

"You can just call me Quist," Walter said. He tipped his head backwards and let out a long howl. The kind of howl I thought only a species of prehistoric wolf could possibly let loose on the world.

Red stepped in front of me, Jack, and Jenny. He tried to get in front of Anne and Leslie, but Leslie looked him in the eyes, and he backed up.

Quist's skin was changing fast. The new skin covered his body almost instantly. He swatted the counter in front of him out of the way with his newly developed paw. He smashed through the wood and old candy as his transformation finished.

He was taller than any of us; he had to squat slightly to move in the store. His fur was bluish gray and covered his lanky limbs. He smashed through a metal shelving unit and let out a howl in our face. He had three rows of teeth. Yeah, three rows; like a shark.

A door behind us flew open and slammed hard. Jack was nowhere to be found.

"Jack," Leslie said with a sigh. She waved a hand backward to us telling us to follow Jack. She stayed behind and faced the wolf down in a staring contest. I wish I could say who won, but I was busy running.

Out back it looked like a junk yard. There were lines upon lines of cars. Quist had to be here hunting for a long time. Jack was standing by a car waving at us. He does not know how to drive. I think given how well he drives while playing video games, theres a good chance we were better off with Quist.

"This one has keys!" he yelled.

We ran in a line against the back wall of the store. Red in front carrying Jenny, Anne and me behind them. An explosion of concrete and dust separated us. When it cleared, Leslie lay on the ground shaking her head in annoyance. Were-Quist stepped through his gas station's new doorway and towered over Leslie.

"Hey!" Jenny yelled as she fought out of Red's grip. "Check the expiration date on this!" It was a really cool thing to say and following it with a silver fork thrown at pro baseball speeds was even cooler. The fork jabbed into the wolf's upper arm. It spun and grabbed the fork, producing heavy smoke from the wound and its hand.

While he was distracted, we all ran to the vehicles. Anne and I hid behind a school bus where we had a hasty conversation about if werewolves should really be able to change during the day.

I was getting ready to start a nice rant about how nothing that had happened so far this weekend was following any sort of rules when Anne covered my mouth.

The bus rocked back and forth as Quist pushed it from the other side. in the distance, I heard a car kick up gravel as it sped away from the station. Anne silently mouthed the words, "they'll come back."

The sound of metal ripping away from metal was enough to make us both jump up and run away fast as we possibly could. Two steps forward and the Stirba's van pulled in front of us.

"Let's go!" Leslie yelled from the passenger window.

Anne and I leaped into the back seat. Leslie took off as fast as a minivan would allow her. We caught up with a blue sedan being driven by Red and followed behind. I looked out of the back window and saw Quist running on all fours. The giant made of tooth and claw was catching up to us a little faster than I cared to think about. I watched it in the mirror like it was a t-rex and my name was Ian Malcolm. Objects in mirrors are closer than they appear.

"Hold on," Leslie said. She whipped the van into the opposite lane and pulled ahead so that she was side by side with the sedan. She rolled down the passenger window and yelled, "Red! That guy is fast! Crud! Midwest monster of the highest grade!"

She slammed on the brakes hard and darted behind the car just narrowly missing a head on collision with an oncoming truck. The truck let loose its horn at what had to be the craziest looking dog the driver had ever seen.

Quist tried to leap the truck, but his back legs caught the gate in the bed. He rolled along the asphalt in a pile of limbs and horror.

I looked back as we peeled further and further away to see the wolf standing up and shaking it off. He was up to a trot before he turned into the woods, and I lost sight of him.

Leslie screamed and swerved; that was really confusing because there was just no way Quist had caught up with us unless he had some sort of teleportation going on. Maybe supernatural monsters and masked killers gain teleportation powers when near a camp? I think it's a theory I could look into more.

I looked out the window on my side and saw what Leslie had swerved around. It was a smaller werewolf running on all four limbs... this one looked more like a sabretooth tiger than a wolf though. I don't know how to explain it, and it didn't make sense at the time.

"Let's just try to pretend that we didn't just almost run over a sabretooth tiger," Leslie said.

"That's so good with me," Anne said. "Were already dealing with werewolves, I don't think I can handle dinosaurs too."

I was glad Jack was in the other vehicle because he wouldn't have been able to resist telling Anne that a sabretooth tiger isn't a dinosaur. It would have been pedantic and pointless; but what is Jack if not someone who pays attention to the small details? Unless it comes to clear Pepsi for some reason.

Both our van and the sedan pulled into the camp with our horns blaring. Ted and Marty came running. We explained what happened at the station. Ted decided he had a revelation and told us to follow. He led us into the cabin that was renovated to keep Marty inside.

"Not a great move," Jack said. "Considering I watched Marty bash his way out of here last night, not a great move."

"I fixed it," Ted said. "I made a fence inside out of some leftover stuff I found outside. Guess what it is? Coated with silver."

"Wait a minute!" Jack yelled. "How did you guys carry the silver?"

Ted grabbed a piece of the fencing and kissed it.

"When we're human, we're a-okay!"

Silverware in the trash mystery was solved.

"How are we getting out when he's in?" Jenny asked.

"Hole in the ground covered by a giant rug," Marty said. "It has a lion printed on it."

"That checks out," Red said.

We walked into the cabin and stood behind the rug. We waited for what felt like forever but also couldn't have been because the sun was still out. If it was the morning when we went to the station, it had to be the afternoon now.

"Listen to that," Jenny said. She pointed toward the tree line in front of the cabin. We all pretended to not notice what was happening. I could sense Quist stalking us on all four limbs. He wasn't so stupid and hungry to not see this was a trap, was he?

He quietly walked up the stairs and into the cabin. A board squeaked, and Jenny took that as a queue to turn and scream like every annoying horror movie girl. Quist raised on two feet and moved toward us fast before vanishing completely from sight.

"Go!" Ted yelled.

We all ran out of the front door as Red slammed it shut and dropped a bar into a locking position.

Quist thrashed around and roared in pain. He would slam against a wall, roar, and then try the other side. The slamming stopped and he started to slow his breathing.

"Alright," a small voice said from inside. I assumed Walter. "I'm willing to talk to y'all."

"What's the deal with chasing us, guy?" I yelled at the closed door. I snapped. I had been changed into a werewolf, chased by multiple werewolves, and now I had to talk to a dumb old man that sold expired food through a closed door.

"You guys are from the government," he said.

"No," Leslie said. "We're from southern Ohio."

"Same thing."

"How did you change in the day?" Jenny asked. She slammed the palm of her hand against the door to put an exclamation point on each word. She was less happy than I was.

"Huh?" Quist asked.

"You were a wolf just now! How! How! How! HOW!"

"I can't do that when I'm a normal old guy."

"Oh," Jenny shrugged and smiled. She looked at the sky and wiped sweat from her brow. "He thinks I said 'howl'"

"No, Quist," Anne said. "How were you a werewolf?"

"Ain't you that TV news reporter lady?"

"Sure."

"Don't you know how to do it yet? You ain't read about them leaves down yonder?"

"I swear," Anne said. She turned to me and pulled a Cow Tail out of her back pocket. "Go get 'im, cowgirl."

I nodded.

"Listen, Quist," I said. "I think you're annoying. I don't appreciate that you sold my friend expired soda. And honestly, you trashed a perfectly good gas station."

"I thought it was all expired?"

I rolled my eyes so hard they must have made a noise that he heard.

"Okay, okay," he said. "I'm sorry about the whole government thing..."

"And you know what?" Jenny said. "I swear I saw a sabretooth tiger run past the car. Dad told me to ignore it... I can't do that. It was too much. It's making my brain throb."

"We were going to ignore the dinosaur too," Anne said.

"Dinosaur?" Jack said. I knew he would do this. When Anne said it, I cringed. I did not want to hear what was about to happen.

"A sabretooth tiger is from the ice age," Jack said. "It isn't a dinosaur at all."

"Oh," Anne said. "I'm sorry. I'm not super into prehistoric stuff."

"I wanted to ignore it," Leslie said. "I didn't want to be in *Jurassic Park* with werewolves."

"This is a major issue," Jack said. "Jurassic Park was about dinosaurs, there wasn't a sabretooth tiger there. I guess maybe there—"

"Jack," Jenny said giving him a patented Stirba death stare.

"Jen... This is a whole thing."

"No, it isn't."

The look she gave Jack was enough to scare me into silence. I know Jack had to feel invisible rays of annoyance piercing his skin. He absolutely had to be melting.

"He has his hand up," Jenny said. She pointed to Quist, who was now standing behind a window with his hand raised. "Let's open the door and hear what he wants to say."

Red opened the door and rolled his eyes. Not the time for a dad joke I guess. There's a first for everything.

"I'm sorry I chased you again," Quist said. "Dante got out, and that makes me really nervous. I love that cat and I can't stand the thought of something happening to him."

"Right," Jenny said. "Because we understand at all why a cat running outside is a big enough deal to try and kill us."

"Dante is a werewolf too. He's the one you're calling a dinosa—."

"Which again," Jack interrupted. "Is the wrong thing to call—"

"Jack," Jenny spoke with so much authority it had a physical impact on Jack and knocked him back a few paces.

"Right," Quist said. "Can I explain?"

"Why not," Jenny said. "We've got nothing but time, I guess. Marsha, can you make sure if the cat that is now a monster and definitely NOT a dinosaur shows up, you tell him to wait just a minute before he kills us? We've got a dialogue to hear, and I have a feeling it's going to be a story. No tangents, please, no side quests, let's just hear it. Spill the beans."

We had to spill our version of the beans with him first and tell him what we were doing up here. Anne suggested that he may be a little confused about being captured by a bunch of werewolves he didn't really know. Kind of made sense why he thought we may have been the government when you think about it.

I refuse to try to recreate that entire dialogue because I hope you've been reading this expose I put together for you, and you can put two and two together about what we told him. If not, that's a you problem, not a me problem. Jenny didn't want any side quests then and I am not going to go on any now; especially not ones that just retread ground we've covered. All you need to know is he thought the Stirba's plan was great; which in turn made me think he had been spending too much time cooped up in a gas station.

After we spilled the beans, Jenny told him open his can.

Quist understood how drastic the situation he was in was and started to spill the beans...

Chapter 17

Roll That Beautiful Spilled Beans Footage

I bought that gas station for ten bucks back in the late eighties. Things were cheaper then; place like that will run you at least fifty now. It ain't much, but it's what I needed to stay where I wanted to stay and to keep an eye on my old camp. I still own the camp, but as you can see... there's a bit of a werewolf problem here. I have yet to find an exterminator that can take care of it.

The truth is I have to keep Dante away from places that others like us tend to frequent. He gets stressed, he changes, he causes a mess I can't clean up, and then he leaves someone else infected. Look at Little Miss TV newscaster. Dante did that... I know you all think it was me, but I can keep my brain pretty well together in most scenarios. Dante just loses it over noise. He's always been that way. When y'all pulled in, I knew we were in for a mess.

I can try and go through it a bit, I don't think it's what that girl called a... what was it? A side quest?

It was this little thing called World War 2, and I had been dismissed. My duty served; I fought for America, made Uncle Sam proud, and was free to go. Unfortunately, a train showing up late ruined my plans for that. Don't you just hate how basically all the plans we make are dependent on someone else? It's life's cruel way of reminding us we have to work together. Bold words from an old fart who lives in solitude.

I was waiting outside by the tracks at a stop. No one was there other than me; which now that I look back was a bit odd. I didn't think the old man who told me to avoid the place at night was serious; ghost stories are important pieces of cultures all over our planet. Did you know most of them are created so that parents could keep their kids away from dangerous places, like a forest at night filled with predators... that's a side quest isn't it? No ghost, no train, just me and Dante's mother.

While I waited for my ride to the air station so I could fly back across the ocean and have a great big homecoming party, I felt watched. You have to understand that I spent most of my time in the war feeling watched; the feeling wasn't anything new to me. I thought my left-over paranoia was playing tricks on me, nothing more and nothing less. I heard the train approaching from miles away; a low rumble that shook the platform, and I could feel it in my bones. As I searched the horizon for lights, I realized the train was behind me and no less than five feet away.

I turned around to see a fur covered thing skulking behind benches and poles. It was trying to hide itself, but it was entirely too large to do so. It walked on four legs; its fur was a dark grey and smelled of meat that had been left outside in April for more than a few days. I covered my nose and coughed. The beast knew I had spotted it and didn't try to hunt anymore. Looking back, as I have many times over these years, I'm not sure why it bothered to hunt. It could have overtook me whenever it wished. I learned later that the feline spirit inside the wolf's body wanted to play with its prey. A cat and mouse situation. Playing with food is how I found myself being dragged through tall grass and across brick roads for miles upon miles.

The thing snatched my upper leg inside its jaws and ran. I remember flying over streams, being carried through darkened alleys lined with bricks. A few times I tried to scream; futile considering the speed I was being carried. No one could have helped me. It was a hopeless situation. Here I had survived horrors I wish to never speak of again; horrors that would not be believed if repeated but were none the less true. Here I was being carried and dragged by a thing I couldn't identify and feared I would never be able to. Would I become another ghost story parents used to keep their kids away from dangerous places?

We approached a circle of wooden wagons fast. I feared maybe some of the experiments I had heard of with genetic manipulation were being proven true, and I was to find myself in the clutches of the enemy. I have never been so thankful for being wrong.

An old woman yelled at the creature. I can't say if the words were in a language I understood at the time or not. I was in shock, and quite frankly being carried like that was exhausting. The beast dropped me and went to the woman's side. It nuzzled its face into her black hair that reached all the way to the ground.

This is how I became a werewolf. I spent years with these people. They taught me how to survive; they taught me how to keep my wolf at bay. Most importantly, they introduced me to the flower and gave me Dante.

When Dante was born, he was the only kitten in the lot born that night who hadn't been spoken for. His mother's name was Ricci, and she was the child of another feline inflicted with this curse. Dante will live much longer than I; his mother is without a doubt still being treated as a queen by those beautiful people. I never discovered if the cats brought the curse, or if the humans accidentally passed it on. I have a theory this is why cats were worshipped in ancient Egypt that I can tell you about later.

I was told of a flower called Garvelle. It is a dark purple in color and grows along the shores of only a handful of lakes in the world. One of those lakes is where the camp that took me in stayed permanently, and another is where I built my new camp. I came back to America with the hopes of finding more like us and showing them that this... change... isn't all bad. We can control it and live a fulfilling life with Garvelle.

I was able to purchase this lake with the money I received from my service. The Army paid me nearly five times what I had earned when they had marked me as missing in action. My girlfriend had moved on and married another former soldier; he was a good man, and I couldn't have hoped for anything better for both of them. It was nothing short of pure agony to discover life had moved on without me. I think we all believe the world works in a linear fashion and only moves when we're present. Hard to imagine other people are living a life the same as you. Both of my parents had passed away before I was able to return. All my friends had assumed I was just another lost life across the ocean.

All of them except one.

My dear friend Leigh Wagner had returned years before me and relocated to Ohio. He offered myself and Dante a place to stay until we could get back on all six of our feet combined. I can guess you've read about the construction of the camp and that's how you knew to come find me, so I'll not waste time on that. I did leave it there in the hopes someone would find it and come seeking my help.

My friend Leigh decided to retire to Florida and sold me that station. It was cheap because I wouldn't allow him to simply give it to me, so we settled for the price of a meal. We've been hiding there since and just watching. It's unfortunate that the canoe race at the camp caused Dante so much stress that he fled.

It was Dante who changed the newscaster, who then changed that man, who then brought you all back here to my door. It is

Dante who is out there in wolf form. We have to find him before he makes my life even more complicated.

Chapter 18

What a Mess, What a Freaking Mess

HAVE YOU EVER TRULY believed your life was being filmed for a movie? I think everyone has had this weird phenomenon happen to them more than once. Some people call it synchronicity when you turn on the radio hoping to hear a No Doubt tune, and that's the first song that plays. They think when these things happen, the universe is telling you that you're on the right path. I think the universe is a director making a movie called *Let's See How Many Weird Things We Can Put Marsha White Through!* Why else would the recreation building choose to burst into flames right after Quist said Dante would make a mess?

"Whoa," Jack said. "Dante's inferno..."

"The movie where James Bond fights a volcano?" Jenny asked

"You betcha."

"No," said Leslie. "That would be *Dante's Peak*. Dante's Inferno is a book about the nine levels of Hell. The same nine levels of Hell it looks like we're going to go through to catch this cat."

"That's not true," Quist said. "He'll just sort of tear stuff up and be a general nuisance. You know... like a cat. We just don't want him to leave here and infect anyone else. I have to fear that if the fire spreads firefighters will arrive."

"Werewolves with axes," Red said. "Cool in concept but terrifying to think about."

"I don't know if I trust a man who can't read expiration dates to tell me the size of a problem," Jenny said. "That whole building is on fire."

It was absolutely on fire, and that was absolutely more than just an average nuisance caused by a cat. Jenny also absolutely tuned Quist out after he said nuisance. Those kinds of things are usually just plates and things being knocked off of counter tops. Maybe a remote pushed under a couch; but never an explosion. We had a cat at home for years that would make eye contact with you before destroying something. I wonder how Dante managed to blow up a building without looking at someone like an arrogant jerk before doing it.

"Oh, actually," Jack said. "That may be my fault. I don't know if I turned the stove off."

When everyone looked at him, he sort of shrugged.

"I found a frozen pizza in there. I thought we would all be hungry."

"I am pretty hungry," Anne said. "But I'm seriously doubting you had time to do that since we've been back."

"It was when you and Marsha were investigating. Jen knew."

"Now don't bring me into all of this," Jenny said. She pointed at Jack. He backed down like lasers were shooting from the tip of her finger.

"Okay," Jack said. "I told her I was thinking about it. But I didn't tell her I followed through."

"Pizza aside," Red said. "The stoves in that building have a shut off if they're left on too long. Jack, you're in the clear on this one."

The movie that is my life theory happened again. The director named Universe flipped a switch and made Dante let out a roar unlike anything I had ever heard. I guess that was supposed to be our queue to know we were getting distracted and heading off on side plots instead of focusing on the main plot line.

Quist decided to take that advice and tell us about Garvelle.

The plant looks like a purple slime along the surface of the lake. It's thin as paper and small as a coin; but when it absorbs water, it stretches and becomes more of a sludge or oil. Stretched too thin... I guess I could relate.

He showed us a purple leaf that he had kept in his pocket. It was the size of a dime, and thin enough that you really couldn't see it lying down. He put it in his mouth and let us watch as it spread across his teeth and tongue. He held up his left hand and began to change into the wolf. His fingers sprouted that weird brownish exoskeleton. It spread down to his wrist. Claws began to burst through the blisters on the tips of his fingers.

He moved his hand in front of his mouth and blew on it as if it were the hottest slice of pizza he could ever hold. The brown began to change to purple and retreat back to the point it had started before completely vanishing. Now I have seen magicians come and go and I have watched a man make an elephant disappear from behind a curtain. These things could all be explained... but I had no explanation for how this worked. I may have tried to debunk it if I wasn't already in a world where werewolves were real. At that point, a UFO filled with sentient chicken tenders could have landed and I would have apologized for how many of their kind I had eaten in my life. I never once feared one of the werewolves was going to dunk me in buffalo sauce before they ate me; so I had to imagine the chicken tender aliens had it pretty bad.

"I can't explain it," Quist said. "I'm no flower scientist or whatever—"

"Etomologist," Jack interrupted. I told you; he can't just leave things alone.

"Sure," Quist gave Jack a thumbs up when he said it. "Somehow it absorbs the change. If you can keep enough in your system; you can feel it moving and control what it covers and what it doesn't."

"Kind of the reverse of the werewolf thing," Anne said.

"This is all getting a bit too *Power Rangers* or something for me," Jenny said. "It works. I can see that. I don't know why I need a science lesson here. I can't tell you how my liver, kidney, heart, or even brain works really... but I use them just fine."

"Not all of them..." Jack said under his breath.

"He's right. I'm using my heart too much when he uses his brain too little or I'd have thrown him up into orbit with the space station by now."

Jack nodded. He knew she was right. Just because he knew that correcting people was annoying didn't mean he was ever going to stop doing it. That was part of his charm; the eternal button pusher.

"Let's just eat a salad of this stuff," Jenny said. "Then we can get Dante, put out that fire, and then sit down and have a completely logical conversation about an illogical subject, 'kay?"

We all nodded; it would have to be 'kay. All of us except Leslie. She nodded, but in a different way. This was a woman who was proud to know she passed down the being terrifying gene to her daughter.

Chapter 19

Get Out of Our Hair, Kid

EVERYONE, AND I MEAN everyone, except Jack, Jen, and I turned into a werewolf and took off like they had rocket skates. If Jack ever sees that I used this reference, he'll lose it. He thinks using the rocket skates in *Toejam and Earl* and going to level zero is cheating. In case you don't know; rocket skates, Icarus wings, or a pool float, go to level one, go through the water all the way to the bottom left of the map. You're welcome.

Red, Marty, and Ted all looked alike as wolves. They were the standard tall and lanky things with blueish grey hair. They had long snouts, stood on two legs, and ran faster than our high school track team if they were melted into a *Sonic-the-Hedge-hog*-shaped running shoe or some other combination of super-fast fictional character and product built for speed... Quist was the same, but his wolf was bigger and somehow looked ancient and primal. Leslie's wolf had dark hair instead of grey. She looked that shade of black that reads as purple to your eyes;

scary stuff if I'm being honest because that means that we could be surrounded by werewolves like her anytime it's dark out; she just blended in. Anne's hair was the same red I knew it would be, but she was the tallest. They all remembered the plans we concocted and didn't waste a second getting started.

Ted and Red; what a duo, right? Maybe they should start a TV series. A buddy cop show about werewolves hunting cryptids; big *X-Files* vibes. The dynamic duo was to run to the burning building and try to find a hose or something. I didn't like their chances. A single garden hose against a burning building sounded like busy work to me. No chance of it working. Jack used to ask me if I thought you could destroy a brick wall with a hot dog if you hit it with it for long enough; Red and Ted were on a hot dog demolition mission if I ever saw one.

Anne and Leslie were heading to a garden shed to find buckets, bowls, bird baths, and whatever else they could fit into the metal cart that Ted left there. They would then fill those up at the lake and be on their way. Picturing two werewolves carrying buckets of water was a great image to have in my mind. Werewolf gardeners... what's next? A werewolf bakery? Actually... maybe there's some money to be made there.

Quist and Marty were there to distract Dante. They would get him stuck in a game of tag and keep him busy. It wasn't tag, but I think it involved running away from Dante more than anything. So, basically the same thing.

The three of us had the task of taking a wheelbarrow to the lake and filling it with as much Garvelle as we could. Pretty simple task. Quist said if we dried it out, Dante would smell it and come running. He would eat it, then he would change back to a cat, and everything would be good. The biggest issue was transporting it safely while water sloshed around.

Sounds like a job you assign kids, right?

The real world isn't like movies. When there's danger like this, it's almost never going to be a situation where the kids have to fix it. I think the adults could sense Jack was scared too. I used my talent for being able to read a situation and decided he was scared when he kept saying, "I don't know, guys. I'm pretty scared of that were-tiger thing."

There we were at the lake picking up chunks of this slimy purple plant. When the Garvelle was out of the water, it seemed to dry up almost instantly and become a normal leaf. Some of it would do the opposite and bloat more before slowly drip drip dripping like that water faucet back home my dad refuses to take five minutes to fix even when the water bill was quadrupled. Really weird process that probably defies the laws of science, but who really cares because wouldn't werewolves deny those same laws? Not my debate, not my essay, not my subject.

"You guys should eat some and see if it works," Jack said. "They didn't tell you not to. I think it's my best idea, honestly."

"They didn't tell us we should either," Jenny said.

"But it helps, right? So, it's probably implied that you eat some. I want to be honest here; between the way Dante changes when he's stressed, the way this is a stressful situation if I've ever seen one, the way you both are werewolves, and the way you both have no control over the werewolf thing... I'm getting a bit anxious."

"I think he's right," I said. I picked up a piece and bit it. It crunched like lettuce, but that's where the similarities stop. Thank the gods of vegetable flavors because other than mustard, lettuce is my least favorite thing. It tasted like the best chocolate, cheese, fried foods and cake I had ever eaten. Not at the same time, but more like a hurricane of flavors. Just one after the other in a process. I think it zoned in on my tastebuds and mimicked my favorite foods. Psychic food—wild time to be alive, man, wild time to be alive.

"I'm not doing that," Jenny said. "It looks gross. Like really gross. Usually I'm not picky; I eat onions and everything. But this looked like snot five minutes ago and I'm not Jack."

Jack rolled his eyes and took a bite of another leaf. He spit it out and made a gagging face.

"Tastes like moldy cheese covered in rotten milk!" he said. "Gross dude!"

"Even Jack doesn't like it," Jenny said. "He's been drinking expired soda this whole time."

"It was your idea," I said. "You said we should eat a salad of the stuff. I don't think it tastes good to him because he isn't... you know—"

"Someone with awful taste?" Jack said. "Marsha, I've watched you eat thousand island dressing. It's disgusting."

I just chose to ignore him. I liked thousand island on cheese-burgers, so what? It tastes like a Big Mac. Better than mustard or lettuce.

"Jenny," I said. "You really should eat it. It helps a lot. I can feel myself in control of the change."

"I guess I should," Jenny said as she picked up a leaf. "Mom and dad will expect me to anyway. Besides, I can't start off our romantic comedy about both of us being werewolves in a circus by telling you no about trying a new food."

"What?" I asked.

"Lost me at the circus," Jack said.

"Happens every time I take him. It's the romantic bit I need more info about."

"Marsha, don't be an idiot, if I can tell you're girlfriends... it's pretty obvious."

"Oh," I said. I couldn't focus on anything but seeing how far I could dig the toe of my shoe into the ground. "That's really cool."

Yeah, I know, great one. This must be part of my charm or something because Jenny smiled, rolled her eyes, blew out a deep breath, and then took a bite of the leaf. Her face went from disgust to enjoyment.

"It really does taste great," Jenny said. "It's like strawberry cheesecake for dessert after BBQ ribs and fries for dinner. Oh! And those cheesy garlic biscuits from Red Lobster!"

Jack picked up another leaf and bit it. He spit it out instantly.

"Yeah," Jack said. "I don't know about that."

The werewolf version of Marty flew overhead at that exact moment. It was strange; life is a movie theory at play here again. He was flying slow and elegantly but also flailing all of his limbs in panic. He splashed into the lake and stayed under long enough for me to worry he may not ever come back up. I was trying to mentally prepare myself to tell my new girlfriend that her brother was probably dead. She would have to live with the realization that she always associates that memory with me until she finally can't take it anymore and leaves me after ten years of marriage. Thankfully, that was when Marty's normal, totally human, not-a-werewolf-at-all head popped up from under the water.

"It's the government!" yelled Quist as he ran behind us in human form and adding to the overall number of moving pieces I was trying to follow.

"What is going on here?" Jack said.

"It's legitimately annoying how those two things happened back-to-back," Jenny said. "I'm about as overstimulated as I can be."

"I don't know what he's going on about," Marty said as he came walking across the shore. "It's his cat. It isn't the government. He's got some sort of paranoid delusional problem, I guess. Dante was chasing us, we thought we lost him, so we paused. He rammed me with the top of his head, I went flying, and here I am. Strong cat. Solid cat."

The trees shook and all I could picture was this sea creature movie Jack had wanted to see.

"That's the ending of *Deep Rising*," Jack said.

"I was trying to remember the name of that movie," I said.

"Did you guys know," Jenny said. "That's actually a King Kong movie? They're on Skull Island at the end and that's genuinely King Kong."

Marty patted her on the shoulder and pointed at the trees.

"There's a big scoop for you, Marsha" Marty said. "I sure hope all that nerdy movie junk can help us get this guy trapped. I guess he could eat the leaves here and change."

"Won't work that way," Quist said from behind us. We all jumped about five feet into the air. "He's gonna have to be inside somewhere or he won't eat it. He'll just think it's a trap and kill us. Sorry about the government thing; old habits and all that."

"No worries," I said. "Jack, you better run for that cabin while we distract him."

"Aw, come on," Jack said, "can't one of you take the wheelbarrow and I can hide? This isn't even right."

Jenny turned her head toward him so fast there was a pop from the breaking sound barrier. She had started the change; her eyes were getting yellow; her teeth were growing.

"Yeah," Jack said. "Okay, I'm going to the cabin!"

I watched him run toward an open door pushing the leaves as my vision went from boring normal human sight to extremely cool werewolf vision. Was I kind of like The Predator? Predator was pretty cool; I think I've mentioned that. Worse things to be like.

Chapter 20

The Chase Scene

WHAT I'M ABOUT TO tell you about will sound like a game show. It probably should be a game show; but unfortunately, I'm allergic to being rich, so I've never pitched the idea. Imagine, a team of five, their goal is to get a wheelbarrow filled with some random thing like grapes to a spot down a hill. One member pushes and runs; the other four protect the pusher from the enemy. The enemy is the boss. Not just any boss; this is the final boss of *Contra*... to be fair I don't know how hard to beat that one is because Level One is as far as I've gotten. Jack says he's beaten it, and I want to talk about how obnoxious of a claim that is... after what I'm about to tell you, I'm going to lay off making fun of him for a bit.

The second time changing was just as thrilling. That exoskeleton thing happened way faster this time and I did feel like a Power Ranger. Quist was right; I was in control of everything after eating Garvelle. The first time, I remembered little bits and pieces, but I was fully conscious this time. I could think clearly and use my heightened senses instead of them using me.

I looked at Jen, and she nodded. She had the same glow I had seen before. Her fur was still a dark blonde with reddish highlights. I wasn't aware enough the first time to notice that. I was impressed a werewolf could even manage stylish highlights, but if one was going to do that, it would be Jenny. We both turned to see Marty and Quist changing again as Dante broke through the tree line.

We must have seen him in a halfway state on the road or just didn't get a good look because here was a ten-foot-tall cat with huge claws and teeth. Dante was a sabretooth tiger mixed with a t-rex. I was horrified.

I turned around to make a motion for Jack to run, but he was already bee-bopping down the hill. The leaves were releasing water and sending it sloshing over the side. Jack, remembering the warning, was trying his hardest to not let the wheelbarrow spill. Every bump the front tire hit he would let out a little yell. One of his yells was so loud it came from behind us.

Thinking that isn't how sound works? It isn't! That scream was Quist's voice while he was running away again yelling about the government. Someone needs to have a conversation with him about the things he sees and thinks are the government. Maybe he's seen some weird genetic experimenting on TV and cannot get past it. It was awful because Dante is HIS cat. Why would he be afraid of HIS cat?

Poor Marty took flight again when Dante swatted him with a paw. The paw was every bit as big as I am in human form. Marty didn't go sky high this time, he just sort of flew and bounced across the lake like a skipping stone.

I didn't have the time to check on him, and neither did Jenny. We both ran toward Jack, we could smell the Garvelle in the air, we could smell the path Jack left behind.

I looked back and Dante was catching up. I didn't know what the plan was, but we had to do something. He would catch Jack in about five seconds flat after he brushed past us like we didn't exist if we couldn't somehow stop him.

I could feel Dante's hot breath; I could feel his feet making the ground shake. It wasn't at all comforting, and I wished I could go back to the reality where kids didn't have to do this kind of thing.

The wheelbarrow hit a bump and flipped over sending Jack rolling forward through the already muddy ground. This was it; I was about to see my best friend get eaten by a were-cat while he tried to over explain how it wasn't a dinosaur. Dante probably wouldn't even notice that Jack was filled with expired soda; poor cat probably lives on a diet of expired food.

Jenny wasn't wasting time picturing Jack getting eaten. She leaped ahead, grabbed him by the back of his pants and threw him forward through the grass and mud like it was the world's biggest slip-n-slide. She grabbed a handful of the leaves and ran toward the trees. Dante turned instantly and chased her.

Great. I would get to see my girlfriend get eaten by a were-cat. What if everyone I ever meet from now on is doomed to be eaten by a were-cat? Am I the angel of death and my flaming sword is actually a cat that lives in a gas station and transforms into a saber-toothed tiger?

I ran behind Dante and Jen as fast as I could. I was on all four limbs using trees and anything else I could plant a foot against for extra momentum. I probably looked pretty cool. They still outran me. I turned corners, jumped creeks, and climbed walls made of stone. They were nowhere.

I gave up. I assumed that if I changed back to human form and sat on a log long enough, something would happen. I was cooked. I was a week-old lasagna on the bottom shelf of a fridge. I put my face in my hands and started to cry. This was all wrong. How could this whole thing have gone so good in so many ways; meeting Jen, meeting Anne... but gone so terribly wrong; sitting on a log crying, everyone I love being eaten, Red's eyesore of a hat.

"Why are you crying?"

I knew the voice. I just couldn't believe it. I looked up, and there she was. I leaped up and hugged her so hard she turned into a Pez dispenser and dropped out one of those candies.

"Easy does it," Jen said. "I'm a human currently. You don't know your own strength. Kind of giving me the ick."

"The ick!" I yelled. "I thought you were dead! And you're worried about how strong I hug you?"

"I just don't want broken cabinets and stuff in my future."

I stared at her. I'm confident a little bit of the Stirba fear emanated from me because Jenny jumped.

"Oh!" she said. "Dante! I dunno... I was running from him, and then he was gone and I was alone. Leaf?"

She held out a piece of Garvelle. Of course I ate it. This time it was the butteriest grilled cheese ever made. It was crispy, gooey, and filled with that yellow cheese that's half plastic probably.

We followed a path back to camp in the perfect direction. It was so perfect that I was convinced that I was actually on a TV show; no more theories, this proved it. When we came from the tree line, the first thing we could see was Jack petting a perfectly normal calico cat.

"He just showed up," Jack said. "I was so nervous. I thought I was dead. I curled up into a ball and then all that happened was a cat jumped on my shoulder. He's kinda cute, isn't he?"

Everyone else showed up then and let out sighs of relief. I asked Quist what his deal with the government was, and he told me he had weird dreams. Jenny told him that didn't cut the mustard and continued to verbally berate him for putting us in this situation.

I shook my head, smiled, and looked at Anne. She gave me a thumbs up, and I returned it.

"What now?" I asked as I looked at the Stirbas hugging each other. Ted and Quist were shaking hands. Jack continued to pet Dante.

"Huh," Anne said. "I think you know exactly what we need to do next, cowgirl."

Epilogue

Live Broadcast

A TV plays the 6 'o clock news in a small diner. The usual things are discussed: this week's political happenings, how much butter will cost next week, what weird new trend a marsupial named Rocko created.

"I got a bill from the school just last week!" Larry says. "They told me Peyton put a paper clip inside a computer and blew it up!"

"It didn't blow up," Joe says. "It just smoked a little."

"Yeah, same thing basically," the man standing behind the counter at the flat top grill says. His name tag says his name is "Ginger," but everyone knows he just really likes old TV shows about people stuck on an island. "Why don't you guys shut up so I can watch this? Supposed to be a big deal."

"Sheesh," Joe says. "Ginger snaps."

On the screen, Anne Ambrose appears with a teenage girl. They're both dressed in the same outfit all the way down to a blazer and pink cowboy boots. They stand in front of what appears to be a summer camp made of wooden cabins.

"I'm here with Marsha White," Anne says. "A young woman who aspires to be a reporter, just like me. I think with what she has uncovered this weekend, I may need to find job ads in the newspaper. I'll hand it over to her."

Anne steps out of frame; the picture zooms in and focuses on Marsha.

"Hello, everyone," says Marsha. "Whether you're at home, out for dinner, or sitting in a bus station; I need you to pay attention. Werewolves are real. I'll allow a pause for laughter.... I know they are because I am one. My friends and I are at Camp Howling where an old werewolf has been hiding for decades, and where two of my friends were bitten, who then spread the werewolfism to me and my close friends. There is a plant here that helps you control the change. This message is for anyone hiding. Come to Camp Howling and we can help you. Now, for everyone who doesn't believe it. Jack, you can zoom out now."

The camera backs up to show a group of six bipedal creatures that can only be described as werewolves standing in a row. The young girl closes her eyes and begins to change. In a few short seconds, there are seven werewolves running across the screen.

Ginger pushes a button on the remote and turns the TV set off. "What a way to promote a movie," he says.

"It isn't for a movie," Joe says. "They really turned into werewolves."

"Yeah?" Larry challenges. "Is that so?"

"Movie effects ain't that good, Larry. It was real."

"Order for Quist," Ginger yells holding a small slip of paper. "How do you want your chicken wings, buddy?"

A man sitting alone in a booth lowers the newspaper he's reading and pets the calico cat sitting next to him. The cat meows in the arrogant way that only a cat who knows it shouldn't be in a diner can.

"Rare," he says.

"That'll kill ya!" Ginger says. "I meant the sauce!"

"Oh, yeah, sorry... how about... Buffalo."

Acknowledgments

Thankee to

Breanna, for listening to me yap at all times.

Mercedes Varnado for inspiring me to be myself.

Emma for making the best covers!

Thank you to Stephanie and Squirm for believing in this book and me!

Thank you to Wendy Pink Horror Dalrymple for not letting me crash out.

Thank you to Joey Powell for helping me brainstorm this idea!

Thank you to whoever you are reading this, and if you've ever helped me in any way!

Write your name here, because you deserve it!

About the Author

Damien Casey is not a werewolf but he thinks being a werewolf would be cooler than being a vampire. You ever see a vampire play basketball? I don't think so.

More YA Reads from Damien Casey!

Mall-ignant

1995 - Millie Lisa goes missing while trying to buy her father a birthday gift at the local mall.

Now - A paranormal research team discovers a hidden floor inside the mall that is stuck in the year 1995. The team sets out to create a viral paranormal video.

What will they find?

A giant cookie determined to destroy them?

A local cryptid?

An invisible jet?

Maybe... what happened to Millie?

Other Titles from Squirm Books

When We Entered That House – Claire L. Smith

Two girls find a Victorian mansion rotting deep in the woods. Something inside doesn't want to let them go...

Hearsepower – Stephanie Sanders-Jacob

Growing up in a funeral home is weird—so is losing your dad. When the hearse Kayla loves takes on a mind of its own, she must decide between her friends, her family, and the last piece of her father she has left.

Skin Deep – edited by Stephanie Sanders-Jacob

A horror anthology featuring the best and brightest authors writing queer Young Adult fiction on beauty and body image.

Available now!

squirmbooks.com